MURDER AND MISFORTUNE

A CLAIRE ROLLINS COZY MYSTERY BOOK 3

J. A. WHITING

Formatting by Signifer Book Design

Proofreading by Donna Rich

To hear about new books and book sales, please sign up for my mailing list at:

www.jawhitingbooks.com

Created with Vellum

For my family with love

CONTENTS

Chapter 1	1
Chapter 2	11
Chapter 3	21
Chapter 4	31
Chapter 5	41
Chapter 6	51
Chapter 7	61
Chapter 8	71
Chapter 9	81
Chapter 10	91
Chapter 11	101
Chapter 12	109
Chapter 13	119
Chapter 14	129
Chapter 15	139
Chapter 16	147
Chapter 17	157
Chapter 18	167
Chapter 19	177
Chapter 20	189
Chapter 21	199
Chapter 22	209
Chapter 23	219
Chapter 24	231
Chapter 25	239

Thank you for reading! 251
Books/Series By J. A. Whiting 253
About the Author 255

1

The early morning fog and humidity hung like a wet blanket in the air making Claire Rollins feel like she was dragging her legs through a lake as she ran the path along the Charles River to the spot where she would meet her running partner and friend, Detective Ian Fuller. Claire and Ian had run a mini-triathlon several days earlier and they were both pleased with their performances and times.

The two had gone out to dinner afterwards to a small restaurant in a cozy inn and although they both tried to ignore it, Claire couldn't deny the sparks that flew between them. Just thinking of Ian sent a warm flutter through her body as she moved her feet swiftly over the path.

There were few other runners out and thirty-five-year-old Claire chalked it up to the day's dense fog making people hit the snooze button on their alarms and turn over for a little more sleep rather than head out to exercise in the damp, dreary day.

A figure approached through the ground-level cloud and for a moment, a flash of nervousness flared in Claire's chest and she gripped tightly to her small canister of pepper spray. As the runner got closer, she could see that it was a woman, similar in size and age to herself. Claire stepped a bit to her right to make more room on the path, and as she and the young woman nodded to one another as they passed, the baseball hat the girl was wearing flew off her head and hit the ground.

Claire stopped, picked it up, and turned to see the person coming back to retrieve the cap. For a moment, Claire and the athletic, dark-haired woman held the hat in their hands at the same time.

"Thanks." The young woman gave Claire a warm, friendly smile, slipped the hat over her head, and turned to continue her run down the trail.

Watching the woman run until she disappeared into the thick milky fog, Claire had an urge to call out to her, but she didn't know why or what she thought she should say. Shaking off a shudder of unease, Claire turned and continued her run in the opposite direction following the bend in the trail until she spotted Ian moving towards her at easy, rhythmic pace.

"Hi." Ian stopped and smiled. His brown hair was damp and a little drop of water fell from a dark strand hanging over his forehead. "Kind of an eerie morning, huh? I wondered if we'd run right past each other in the fog and not even notice."

Claire returned the smile and as she tucked a loose piece of her long, curly blond hair back into her ponytail, she looked over her shoulder to the trail behind her. "It was weird running alone through the mist. It made me uneasy."

Ian looked down at her hand and nodded. "You've got your pepper spray with you. Good."

They took off together and when the path led in two different directions, they veered to the left to stay along the river. Ian chattered as they ran talking to Claire about keeping up their training, finding another mini-marathon to do, and reminding her that she'd promised to run the Boston Marathon with him if they both achieved their personal goals in the last event.

"We have to qualify for Boston, you know," Claire said. "Why don't we plan to do the Marine Corps Marathon in D.C. as a qualifying run."

"Why that one?" Ian asked.

Claire grinned. "I heard it's a flat course."

Chuckling, Ian said, "If we get involved with a charitable organization and raise enough money, we can run Boston with the organization's group and then we don't need to complete a qualifying race."

"Good idea." Claire extended her leg to jump over a puddle. "But, I still might need more convincing to work towards a marathon. We're both busy and besides, training during the winter will be awful."

Tabling the discussion for the time being, they ran the final three miles and ended at a small parking lot where Ian had left his car. "Do you want me to drop you at your townhouse or at Tony's market?"

Claire looked back at the trail through the mist, as something unpleasant picked at her.

"Claire?"

She turned her blue eyes to Ian, blinking. "What did you say?"

"Is something wrong?" Ian's voice held a tone of concern.

No." Claire shook her head trying to throw off the annoying sensation she was feeling. "Nothing's wrong."

"Why do you keep looking at the path?"

"I'm not." Claire knew she kept looking at the path, but she didn't know why. Something about that girl who dropped her hat kept pinging in her brain and she had a compelling urge to rush back to where they'd briefly met. "I'm looking at the fog. It makes everything seem mysterious."

"Well," Ian kidded, "should we stay longer to admire the landscape or should we leave so we can get to work and not get fired?"

"I like working at Nicole's chocolate shop." The corner of Claire's mouth turned up. "I don't want to lose my job. Let's go." Just as she was about to get into Ian's car, images of the woman runner flashed in her mind and for a moment, her throat constricted and she couldn't suck in a breath. Coughing to mask her momentary discomfort, Claire slid into the vehicle with the beginnings of a headache pounding in her temple.

~

Claire and Nicole put the finishing touches on the vegetable lasagna they'd spent the past hour and a half making and Claire slid it into the oven and set the timer. Nicole went to the closet to get the dogs' leashes and when the Corgis saw what she was doing, they began to dance around the kitchen eager to leave the townhouse for a walk.

The fog had lifted around noon revealing a bright, cloudless blue sky and an afternoon breeze off the ocean had cleared out the heavy humidity. Claire, Nicole, and the dogs left the house and headed through the Beacon Hill neighborhood streets down to the path that ran along the river. Walking the trail that led to the path Claire ran on that morning caused a shiver of worry to race through her as she remembered the young woman who passed her and dropped her hat.

Nicole chattered about the people she'd interviewed for the waitress job at the chocolate shop. "I just don't know. I'm not sure any of them will fit in. I have two more to talk to tomorrow."

"You'll find the right person," Claire told her.

They walked the dogs to the small wooded park located off of the river path and freed them from their leashes so they could dart around sniffing the grass and trees. Claire and Nicole settled on a bench facing the water and watched the people strolling by and the runners jogging past.

"When I went to meet Ian this morning, it was so foggy I could hardly see where I was going. There weren't many people out. It felt sort of weird running through the mist."

With a worried look, Nicole shifted on the seat to better face her friend. "Did something happen?"

"No." Claire sighed. "I don't know why I felt so odd. Maybe it was the spooky atmosphere of the fog."

Nicole narrowed her eyes. "*Nothing* happened? Nobody spoke to you? Nobody bumped into you? You didn't sense anything?"

Claire looked out at the boats on the river. "A girl, maybe a little younger than us, ran by me. She had a baseball hat on. A gust of wind came up and blew it off. I picked it up and handed it to her."

"Then what?" Nicole asked warily.

"Then I ran to meet Ian."

"What about the girl?" Nicole's gaze was intense.

"I didn't see her again."

"Claire," Nicole said with a tone of seriousness, "did you have some sensation? Was your *intuition* trying to tell you something?"

"I don't know what it was." Claire reached up and twisted a long lock of her hair. "I kept wanting to look down the path. Something felt off. I don't know why, but I wanted to talk to that girl. It seemed urgent."

Claire had recently developed the ability to sense or pick up on things about people especially if she touched the person or something the person owned. The skill had come in handy during the past six weeks when she and Nicole had been drawn into two difficult mysteries.

Claire gave a shrug and smiled. "Maybe I shouldn't run in fog."

Nicole continued to question Claire. "Did you feel something when you handed the runner her hat?"

"Now that I'm thinking about it, I suppose what I felt couldn't have had anything to do with her." Claire wasn't so sure the interaction didn't hold some importance, but she wanted to forget the whole thing so she tried to convince herself it was nothing.

"Good." Nicole sat back against the bench and turned her face to the sun. "Let's talk about something else. How about those cream cheese brownies you were telling me about? Want to make some tomorrow and see how they go over with the customers?"

"Sure." Claire switched her attention to chocolate and desserts. "I think they'll be a hit."

"Do you have any other ideas for new sweets we can add to the menu?"

Claire made some suggestions and while she listened to Nicole's opinions, she noticed someone walking along the path near the water with a young man and she sat up straight, her eyes wide.

Feeling Claire's sudden movement, Nicole shaded her eyes with her hand. "What are you looking at?"

"Over there." Claire gestured and let out a sigh of relief. "It's the girl I saw on the path this morning."

A young woman with a long dark ponytail wearing shorts and a t-shirt and a baseball hat on her head walked along beside a tall, slim man with dark blond hair. The man had on a short-sleeved t-shirt that showed the muscles in his arms.

"She looks fine," Nicole said. "So your *feeling* must have been from the foggy weather, like you said."

"Yeah." Claire nodded. "I have to admit that I worried about her. I'm glad to see that she's okay."

"Now you can transfer your attention to the chocolate shop menu." Nicole checked her watch. "The lasagna will be ready soon. We should head back."

Claire called to the dogs and Bear and Lady dashed over to the bench wagging their tails. She hitched the leashes onto their collars and handed one of them to Nicole and they started on their way out of the park.

Lady hesitated, turned around to look at the walking path near the river, and let out a whine. Claire's heart rate sped up when she saw what the Corgi had her eyes on.

The dark-haired runner with the baseball hat had turned around and was strolling back up the walkway with her companion. The earlier feeling of unease wrapped around Claire like a vise and would not let go.

2

Before going to work at Nicole's chocolate shop, Claire and the Corgis, heading to Tony's Market and Deli, walked along the brick sidewalks of Adamsburg Square, a small neighborhood consisting of a few blocks at the edge of Beacon Hill. The early morning sun's rays promised another hot, humid day for the city of Boston.

Bear and Lady wagged their tails, sniffed at the base of light posts and at spots on the brick walkways, and jauntily trotted in front of their owner. The dogs knew the routine and looked forward to staying with Tony in the store or lounging in the small, walled-in grassy space off the market's store room while Claire was at work.

Claire carried a large pastry box full of different

versions of the cream cheese brownies she and Nicole had discussed the previous day. There was an upcoming food festival that would take place near the city's waterfront which would feature various chefs, restaurants, and dessert shops. A contest would be held that day to vote for and choose the best items entered into different categories.

Nicole wanted to feature the chocolate shop by setting up a booth to serve pastries to festival goers, but more importantly, she wanted to enter a dessert in the food contest's pastry category and she'd been discussing possible options with Claire.

Inside Tony's market, Claire joined retired State Supreme Court Justice Augustus Gunther at their usual table. There were only three small tables tucked in a corner of Tony's place near the coffee and tea station he'd set up alongside some muffins and donuts for customers who wanted to run in for a quick takeout item.

Augustus already had his first coffee of the day on the table in front of him. The dogs rushed over for their morning pats and they wiggled around the older judge like they hadn't seen him in years.

"You're early." Claire set the pastry box on the table before going to get her tea. "Where's Tony?"

"He's taking some recycling items to the bins out

back," Augustus said and eyed the brown box. "What do we have here?"

Tony Martinelli, in his early seventies, tall, tanned, and stocky with a head of white hair, came in through the store room and the dogs hurried to greet him just as they'd done with Augustus.

Opening the pastry box, Claire explained to Tony and Augustus about the food festival and Nicole's plan to enter something into the contest. "So I made these cream cheese brownies as our first option. They're all basically the same, but I've divided them into three batches and added some secret ingredients to them. I'd like you to sample the three different kinds and give your opinion on the taste."

Tony carried over paper plates so Claire could arrange the three different flavors on separate dishes.

"I won't tell you the flavors. I don't want to feed into your preconceived notions of what you like and don't like. Try them and let me know what you think." Claire folded her arms on the table and leaned forward. She said to Tony, "Maybe I could bring in a platter of desserts and some of your customers can vote for their favorites."

Tony reached for one of the brownies. "That'd be

fine with me as long as I get to eat more of them. I'll move stuff around on the front counter so you can set up your platter where the customers can see it." The big man bit into the sweet treat, chewed, and swallowed.

Claire watched him with wide eyes.

Tony took another bite, savored it, and swallowed.

"Well?"

"Don't rush me." He raised his index finger. "I'm giving this serious thought." Tony went through the process with each of the brownie flavors taking his time with the taste test.

Claire gestured to the dishes. "Augustus? Would you like to share your opinion?"

"I would indeed. I'm so fascinated with Tony's process, I got distracted." The slender man was dressed in his usual manner. Today's fashion variation had the judge wearing a light blue summer suit, white starched shirt, and a dark blue tie. He removed three of the brownies and placed them on his plate.

"I've made my choice," Tony announced as he licked the tip of his finger.

"Wait," Claire admonished. "Let Augustus make

a decision before you tell him which one is your favorite. You're not allowed to influence him."

Tony folded his arms over his chest and watched the man bite and chew.

"I have made my choice." Augustus dabbed his lips with a paper napkin. "All three are delectable, but this is my favorite." He pointed.

"That's the one with toasted coconut." Claire looked pleased.

"Nope," Tony said. "That was my least favorite." He pointed to a stack of brownies on the plate in the center of the table. "I liked these the best."

Claire nodded and said, "Those have caramel swirl. Why didn't you like Augustus's favorite?"

"I don't like coconut." Tony went to the front of the market he'd owned for fifty years to wait on a customer.

"What about these? What secret ingredient is contained in these brownies?" Augustus asked.

The young woman grinned. "Marshmallow."

"I almost chose the marshmallow flavor as my number one." Augustus raised his coffee mug. "Well done, Claire. Any of these brownies would be grand prize winners."

Claire thanked the judge. "We'll have other things we'd like you and Tony to try. I'll bring some things in most mornings until we decide which bakery sweet will be our contest entry."

"Well, I can look forward to that." Augustus nodded his snow white head in approval and patted his waist. "At my age, I have trouble keeping weight on. These wonderful desserts will be good for me." The judge was over ninety years old and he had a very slim frame.

Claire chuckled. "There aren't many people who have that problem."

"What will you bring in next?" Augustus asked, his light blue eyes sparkling with interest.

"We were thinking of some custard flans. What do you think of that?"

"I adore custard." Augustus's eyes closed for a moment. "My dear grandmother made the most delicious custard pie. I can practically taste it just thinking about it."

Claire took on a look of mock-horror. "You told me your grandmother was a magnificent baker. My confidence just went out the window."

Tony called from the deli counter. "Hey, Blondie, could you bring some of those brownies over here? A few customers want to help out and give their opinions."

Carrying the platter to the front, Claire passed

the squares around to the three early morning customers and waited for their comments. An older woman gave her the idea to try using melted Aztec chocolate in the brownies.

Claire listened as the people told her what they loved and what they thought might improve the sweets. Looking up at the clock, she said, "Oh, no. I have to hurry or I'm going to be late for work."

She thanked everyone for their input and promised more pastries to try over the next few days as she and Nicole narrowed down the item that would be their entry at the upcoming festival.

Claire said goodbye to her dogs, wished Augustus a nice day, hugged Tony, and hurried out the door into the warmth of the early summer morning. July's white hot sun rose over the soon-to-be bustling city and the air was heavy and still.

Deciding to take a shortcut, Claire walked up a cobblestoned alley that ran behind a quiet street of brownstone houses. She took a right onto a small lane that led to the main thoroughfare that passed in front of the State House and snaked through the city into the North End.

Ingredients, recipes, and the new twists they could put into bakery items in order to produce something new and distinctive swirled around in the young woman's mind and she thought of some suggestions to share with Nicole as soon as she arrived at the chocolate shop.

Claire noticed a small, dark, compact car parked at the corner up ahead. The lane was small and skinny and it wasn't a good place to leave a vehicle. She could hear the car's engine running.

A buzzing sense that something was wrong started in her chest and spread out through her body like an alarm growing louder and louder. Claire glanced around. No one was in sight. Her heart pounded.

The idea of turning around and taking a different way to work zipped in her head, but she took in a deep breath and told herself she was being foolish. She tried to convince herself it was just a parked car stopped for a minute at the side of the street.

As she got closer, Claire's heart pounded and sweat beaded up under the hair on the back of her neck. The sense of foreboding was so strong that she crossed to the other side of the road and quickened her pace.

As she walked parallel to the vehicle, she had the sensation of a reddish light exploding in her brain like a firecracker going off next to her head. Adrenaline rushed through Claire's body and she stopped short, turning to stare at the dark car. The street was still deserted and quiet, except for the sound of the running engine. Breathing a sigh of relief, Claire realized she must have imagined the light and sound.

Or did she?

Claire's hands began to shake and a wave of fear gripped her. The glare on the car's windows made it hard to see if anyone was inside.

Stepping off the sidewalk onto the street, Claire inched towards the vehicle.

One step, two steps.

When she was close to the passenger side, she bent a little at the waist to take a quick look through the car's open window.

Letting out a yelp, her heart dropped into her icy, cold stomach as she turned her back to the car, her hand over her mouth. She shut her eyes for a moment, but had to open them right away because the awful image of what she'd seen burned in vivid color against her closed eyelids. Feeling like she might retch, Claire rubbed at her forehead with the palm of her sweaty hand.

It couldn't be, she must be mistaken. Forcing

herself to pivot around to take another look, a gasp escaped from her throat.

The young woman she'd seen on the running path yesterday sat slumped in the driver's seat, her head at an odd angle. An angry, red bullet hole marked the center of her forehead.

Claire blinked and for a full minute, she stood weak in the street staring in disbelief, her shoulders slumped, her arms limp and hanging down by her sides.

Momentarily pulling herself out of the fog of shock, she fumbled in her bag for her phone, placed the "911" call, and waited next to the car not wanting the dead young woman to be alone.

Why did this happen? Why?

3

When the police arrived, they questioned Claire and took a statement from her. She called Ian who was at a conference in Connecticut and told him what had happened and he talked to her for a long time trying to offer some comforting words. When Claire explained that she thought she recognized the woman from her run on the trail the other day, Ian suggested that maybe she was mistaken since the fog was so thick Claire might not have gotten a good look at her.

Claire knew it was the same person, but she couldn't tell Ian the reason she was so sure about it was because she had a strong, special intuition so she agreed with him that the dead woman probably wasn't the person she saw running.

When Claire arrived at the chocolate shop for her shift, Nicole took one look at her friend and knew something was terribly wrong. "Now what's happened?"

Robby, Nicole's part-time employee, hadn't arrived yet so the two women could talk freely about the morning's discovery. Shaking like a leaf, Claire slumped in a chair and gave the terrible news of her unfortunate walk to work. "It's the same woman I saw on the running path. I'm sure of it."

Nicole let out a long, drawn-out sigh. "Here we go again. We just finished the Dodd mystery and now this." She crossed her arms and rested them on the table. "I know what you're thinking. That you should have warned this woman you sensed she might be in danger." Nicole cocked her head. "You know doing that was an impossibility. You can't walk up to a stranger and say something like that."

"What should I have done?" Claire's eyes glistened with tears.

"Nothing." Nicole was adamant. "Think about it realistically. There isn't anything that could have been done. Nothing. We don't like it, but that's the way it is."

Claire's sad expression showed that she didn't like her friend's answer.

"People would never accept you telling them they're in danger. You'd come off like a crazy person." Nicole shrugged. "Let's talk about what we *can* do something about."

Claire shook herself and sat up straight. "Okay."

"Your skill and our digging can help find the bad guys," Nicole said encouragingly. "Most of the time things can't be prevented, but when they do happen, we can step in and help out. The past two times, we've been able to help bring perpetrators to justice." She paused and held Claire's eyes. "Your skill can bring a measure of peace to the victims and their families. Those are the things we can do, so let's get on with it."

The corners of Claire's mouth turned up slightly and she gave a nod. "Okay. You're right."

Nicole's tone was all business when she said, "Tell me everything about this woman. Tell me again about the day you saw her in the fog and then tell me again about this morning."

Claire laid out the details of her brief interaction with the girl on the running trail and then explained again about seeing the car and the woman inside of it. "We'll have to wait for the news reports or maybe Ian will be able to tell us who she is ... who she *was*."

Nicole added, "And where she lived, worked, all that stuff."

"We saw her walking by the river with that guy. Remember?"

"Yes," Nicole said, "tall, slim but with a muscular build, dark blond hair."

"Boyfriend?" Claire suggested.

"Maybe. He could be a friend or a brother, maybe a neighbor?"

Twenty-one-year-old Robby, a talented vocalist and music student, opened the door and entered the shop and when he saw Claire and Nicole sitting around instead of preparing for the day, he gave them the eye. "What's the pow-wow about?"

"We're going over ideas for our food festival entry," Nicole fibbed.

"Right." Robby's blue eyes looked skeptical. "What's it *really* about?"

"Okay, I'll tell you the truth." Nicole's face was serious. "We're discussing your recent poor performance here at work."

"Now I know you're lying." Robby headed to the backroom humming a show tune.

"You want to go home?" Nicole asked Claire gently. "After the morning you've had, it might be best if you go home and take it easy."

Claire stood up. "Thanks, but I need the distraction. It's better to stay here with you and Robby and keep busy."

They got to work and the morning flew by as a steady stream of customers came and went so quickly that Claire, Robby, and Nicole barely could catch a breath.

When Ian called in the afternoon, Claire took the call out front on the sidewalk.

"Secret phone calls?" With a raised eyebrow, Robby questioned Claire when she came back inside. "What's the mystery?"

Claire took a glance at Nicole and her friend nodded. "We may as well tell you."

Since all the customers sitting at the tables in the shop had been waited on, the three headed to the backroom where Claire explained what had happened that morning and how she saw the woman running the previous day.

"Well, heck." Robby's mouth dropped open and his blue eyes lost their sparkle.

"I was on the phone with Ian. The woman has been identified. Her license was in her wallet in the car."

"Then it wasn't a robbery?" Robby asked. "Her wallet was still in the car?"

"It doesn't seem to be a robbery. The woman's name is Ashley Smith, twenty-nine. She lived in an apartment on Beacon Hill." Claire looked at Nicole. "With her boyfriend."

"That guy we saw with her yesterday must be the boyfriend." Nicole asked, "Does Ian know where she worked?"

"She was an account manager at a downtown firm," Claire said. "Pennington Private Wealth Management."

"The woman must have known her stuff." Robby sniffed. "That's a fancy pants financial services company. They wouldn't give any small fish like us the time of day."

Actually, Claire was well-acquainted with the management firm. Almost two years ago, she had inherited quite a large sum of money from her late husband, but only Nicole was privy to that fact having recently learned the information from Claire.

"So could this shooting be related to something going on at the firm?" Nicole asked. "Or was it purely random with Ashley being in the wrong place at the wrong time?"

"Good questions." Claire's mind raced thinking about who she might contact at the financial services firm to find out some information about the former employee.

"Does Ian know the boyfriend's name?" Robby asked.

Claire gave a nod. "Michael Burton. He works at the same firm."

Robby straightened. "Wait a minute. I know a Sally Burton. She goes to school with me. This guy must be her brother. I met him once at a production we were in. Michael ... yeah, Sally told me he worked at that big-shot financial place."

Well." Nicole narrowed her eyes. "This could come in handy."

Claire was thinking the very same thing. "Your friend probably knew Ashley, or at least, had met her."

"Want me to text Sally?" Robby asked.

"No," Claire said forcefully. "She might not know what's happened. Or if she does know, she's probably in shock. Don't contact her yet. Wait."

"Right. What am I thinking? I'll see her at school. Maybe I can talk to her then." Robby went out front to check on the customers.

"I know someone who works at that firm." Claire kept her voice down.

Nicole smiled. "Perfect. That seems like a good

place to start. Find out if there's a sensitive account Ashley was working on."

"If nothing else, maybe I can find out what the woman was like." A dark frown pulled at Claire's lips.

"What are you thinking?"

Claire lifted her eyes to her friend. "There's an odd feeling swirling around this woman's death. I don't know what it means."

"Yet." Nicole smiled.

Claire rested her chin in her hand. "I think you have too much faith in my ability to sort things out."

"You haven't failed me yet." Nicole gave Claire a playful poke.

"Speaking of which," Claire wanted to change the subject since there didn't seem to be anything more that could be said about the new case. "I brought some brownies to Tony's market this morning to get some opinions on the different flavors."

"You were very busy this morning, weren't you?" Nicole observed trying to lighten the mood.

"There wasn't a specific standout. Each flavor had about the same number of votes," Claire reported. "Of course, it was a small sample size. I was thinking we should cut small pieces and have the customers here taste them for free and vote. We could set up a table in the front of the store."

"I like it. Let's start the taste-test the day after tomorrow. Having the customers involved will create some buzz about us being in the competition and maybe it will encourage them to go and support us." Nicole winked. "We don't want the wrong pastry shop to win the prize."

Something Nicole said caused a shot of anxiety to race through Claire's body, but she had no idea what it was and she tried to push the feeling away by asking, "Want to start with the brownies or the custard flans?"

"How about the brownies? We can gather the input and then the next day do the custards. Let's try seven or eight days of different desserts and the one with the highest rating will be our entry."

"Sounds good." Claire nodded as a feeling of fatigue flooded through her muscles. It seemed that the reality of discovering the woman in her car was just starting to hit her. "I'll start some dough for tomorrow morning, then I'll head out to Tony's to pick up the dogs."

Nicole gave her friend a hug, told Claire to call anytime of the day or night if she needed anything, and then headed to the front of the store. "Try not to worry," she said as she was about to leave the room. She knew Claire felt a heavy duty to help figure out what happened to the young woman in the car. "We'll put our heads together. It'll all work out."

As Claire took the flour, sugar, and butter out of the cabinets to prepare some batter, her phone dinged with a missed call and when she saw who it was from and listened to the voicemail, her heart started to race.

It was from Bradford Bilson, a senior vice president at Pennington Private Wealth Management, someone she'd met only a handful of times. In his message, he asked her if she could meet in regards to Ashley Smith. *I was very sorry to hear you were the one who found Ms. Smith this morning.*

How does Bradford Bilson know I found the woman? And what exactly does he want to talk about?

4

Bradford Bilson sent a car to pick up Claire for their meeting. She had the driver meet her in front of the State House not wanting the car to come to her home even though she knew Bilson would just have to pick up a phone and ask someone at the firm to look in their files for Claire's address. Still, she preferred to keep her financial life and her personal life separate ... as much as she possible could.

Claire wore her long, curly hair slicked back into a bun and had huge, black- rimmed sunglasses on. Her black skirt hit two inches above the knee and her suit jacket fit like a glove. A crisp, snow white shirt showed under the jacket.

Whenever she visited the firm to meet for her quarterly account updates, she dressed professionally and acted the part of a ... well, the part of a person in the social class her money had landed her, but in an echelon she felt she had no business being in.

Claire had grown up dirt poor. She'd worked like a dog in school, did extremely well, and went on to graduate from a prominent law school which resulted in meeting and marrying Teddy Rollins, one of the wealthiest men in America.

Claire always felt that people in Teddy's circle snickered at and whispered about her. *Gold digger. Social climber. Moneygrubber.* When Teddy died, some of his greedy business acquaintances tried to wrest the company and wealth from her, but she surprised a number of people when she battled back and won.

Teddy loved Claire and she'd loved him. He left everything to her and she made darned sure his wishes were honored.

Bradford Bilson asked Claire to meet him on his yacht in Boston Harbor preferring their conversation to have maximum privacy. Why it was necessary to talk on a boat puzzled Claire, but she agreed to it out of curiosity.

The driver pulled the silver Mercedes into a parking space and a man in a nautical-type uniform escorted Claire down the docks to the metal walkway that led to the massive three-story yacht. Claire paid close attention to the planks on the walkway so her heel wouldn't catch and send her sprawling. That wasn't the kind of entrance she was hoping for.

The stern of the boat had a large covered deck area furnished with teak and white cushioned furniture. The escort slid back a glass door and gestured for Claire to enter. She nodded and stepped into a fabulous sitting room with gleaming wood on the floors, the trim, and halfway up the walls.

Huge vases of fresh flowers sat on several tables scattered around the space. Glass windows on two walls looked out over the harbor, plush area rugs were underfoot, and expensive cream furniture completed the presentation of wealth and elegance.

Bradford Bilson stood before Claire in a fitted, dark blue suit, white shirt, and red tie. A bit of gray showed at the temples of his medium brown hair. In his mid-fifties, the man had a wide forehead, close set, pale blue eyes, and a long, sharp nose. His bearing gave the impression that he was a man of authority, someone important, someone who got his way.

"Claire, a pleasure. Thank you for coming."

Bilson shook her hand. "Please have a seat."

The handshake was so brief Claire didn't have a chance to pick up on anything from Bilson.

The two sat side by side in nautical blue chairs with a glass and pewter table between them. A uniformed man arrived in the room, Claire didn't know where he came from, carrying a small silver tray with glasses of white wine and a platter of fruit, a dish of nuts, and a selection of cheese and crackers. He placed the snack items and the two wine glasses on the table and then disappeared.

"I heard you had quite the unpleasant experience the other morning." Bilson sipped his wine. "I was very sorry ... shocked, to be honest, to hear about the death of our firm's associate, Ms. Smith."

"Yes. It was horrible." Claire offered condolences for the loss of his employee.

"Can you tell me how you happened upon the vehicle and what you saw?" Bilson kept his face looking sincere and concerned.

The part of the question about what Claire had seen seemed intrusive and inappropriate. "May I ask why you'd like to know?"

"Ashley Smith worked for us for several years. She was an impressive talent. We're simply concerned for our employee."

"Did you know Ashley well?" Claire asked.

"Not well, no. We'd met several times, but I receive updates and information regarding the associates, how they're doing, what needs improving, what they excel at. I felt I knew Ms. Smith. She was part of our firm's family."

Claire never liked men like Bilson ... an air of superiority, well-spoken and articulate, but never saying much of importance, a well-cultivated air of sincerity which was often just a phony façade. "Ms. Smith was an account manager with the firm?"

"She was. Doing very well. She was a rising star." Bilson nodded and clasped his hands together with his forefingers pointing to the ceiling. "How did you find her? How did you come upon the car?"

Claire had no intention of revealing that she was employed in a chocolate shop and was on her way to work so she said, "I was out for an early morning walk. I saw the car parked at the curb. I passed by, and ... there she was."

"Did you know Ms. Smith?" Bilson asked.

Claire was surprised by the question. "No, I didn't."

"Were there signs that the car had been vandalized?"

"How do you mean?" Claire tilted her head in

question.

Bilson gave a shake of his head. "Were the side windows broken?"

"No. The windows were down."

"Did you notice if anything looked like it had been stolen? Were the contents of her purse on the floor of the car? Was there a purse in the vehicle at all?"

"I didn't see a purse, but that doesn't mean there wasn't one in the car. I didn't linger very long to notice. I saw Ms. Smith, backed away. I called the police."

"Were you there when the police did the preliminary inquiry?"

"I stayed at the scene until the police arrived and I left after giving a statement and answering some questions."

"Did you happen to hear anything?"

"Hear anything? Like what?"

"What the investigators were saying about the crime."

"No." Claire gave her head a firm shake. "I didn't hear anything. I wasn't paying attention to what they were saying. Why don't you ask the police these questions?"

"We have. They aren't forthcoming. It's an active

investigation and they aren't sharing information."

"That's understandable. Why do you want to know these things?" Claire asked the man. "What bearing does it have on the firm?"

A shadow passed over the man's face. "It could have quite a lot of bearing."

Claire eyes widened and she squared her shoulders. "Do you suspect someone at the firm of having something to do with Ms. Smith's murder?"

Bilson's eyebrows shot up at the question. "No, no. Not at all."

Claire leveled her eyes at the man. "What about a client? Are you worried that one of your clients might have had a hand in this?"

Bilson hesitated for a moment. "No. I can't imagine such a thing."

"Then what could the murder have to do with the firm?" Although Claire was getting impatient, she kept her voice even. "What are your concerns? Why did you ask to speak with me?"

"Because our employee was killed." Bilson shifted in his seat and reached for his wine glass. He took a long sip and set it back down on the table. "Financial institutions have far-reaching associations, a web of people criss-crossing in many directions. A firm is only as good as its reputation."

Claire marveled at Bilson's practiced ability to dodge a direct question with an indirect reply. "So you worry that one of your associates or connections has something to do with Ashley Smith's murder."

"I'm only trying to gather information. To be proactive. We all cared very much for Ms. Smith."

Claire held the man's gaze.

After several seconds, Bilson let out a long sigh. "We're concerned with what Ms. Smith might have been involved in and how that might reflect on our institution."

"Were there any indications that Ashley was mixed up in something illegal?"

"Not to our knowledge."

"Was she working on a sensitive case?"

"That wouldn't be unusual. Many of our clients and cases need to be handled with care and discretion." Bilson's pale blue eyes were like lasers on Claire. "You live in the Beacon Hill area, correct? Adamsburg Square. Had you ever run into Ms. Smith? Do you recall seeing her in the neighborhood?"

A shiver ran along Claire's skin and not knowing why, she made the decision not to reveal having seen the woman running on the path by the river. "I didn't know her."

Bilson cocked his head slightly. "That's odd, since you lived in the same neighborhood."

"It's a popular and populated part of the city," Claire said. "People come and go all the time. Tourists visit every day. I don't know and haven't even met the majority of people on my own street."

"A downfall of modern living, I suppose."

Claire didn't respond.

Bilson changed the subject and smiled. "You've been happy with Cameron Gannon's handling of your accounts?"

"Very much so," Claire told him.

"Excellent." Bilson nodded and leaned forward about to stand up. "Well, I appreciate you coming to speak with me." The meeting had obviously come to a close. "Too bad it was under such unfortunate circumstances."

"Why did we meet here on the boat?" Claire remained sitting. "Why not at the office?"

"Some discussions are better suited to a more private environment."

Claire and Bilson stood at the same time.

"How did you know that I found Ashley's body?" Claire watched the man's face.

A momentary break in Bilson's composure flickered over his face, but his experience kicked in and he responded smoothly. "Word came through several associates. I don't know who the initial person was who brought the information to our attention."

Claire didn't believe it and this time when they shook, she placed her free hand over their locked hands for a moment in a gesture of compassion in order to try and sense what she could from the man. He walked her to the sliding glass door where the uniformed employee stood waiting.

Claire and Bilson exchanged goodbyes and she followed the escort to the metal walkway that would take her to the dock. For most people, the meeting would have felt like a waste of time with nothing of importance coming from it.

But Claire wasn't *most people* and her interaction with Bilson could not have been categorized as a waste. When she shook hands with him, little zaps of electricity pulsed into her skin and she sensed that the senior vice president was not being fully forthcoming with her. He was concerned about what had happened to Ashley Smith, but more so than what seemed appropriate in an employee-employer situation.

Bilson was worried about something.

Very worried.

5

Claire got in touch with her financial advisor, Cameron Gannon, at Pennington Wealth and asked him to meet her early in the morning at a coffee shop in Charlestown. When he asked what she wanted to discuss so that he could prepare whatever she needed, Claire told him it had nothing to do with her accounts and that she hoped he could keep the fact of their meeting in confidence.

The coffee shop was located near the Navy Yard, which in its hey-day was a bustling shipbuilding facility of the United States Navy. Closed in 1974, the area was transferred to the National Park Service and anchored one end of the Boston Freedom Trail.

The Freedom Trail runs through the city passing locations important to United States history ... graveyards, churches, the site of the Boston massacre, Faneuil Hall, the Paul Revere House, and the USS Constitution, a wooden-hulled, three-masted frigate of the US Navy launched in 1797 and named by President George Washington.

The coffee shop had photographs of historical sites framed and hanging on the walls. Claire loved history and enjoyed looking at the pictures while she waited for Cameron to arrive.

The thirty-four-year-old financial advisor hurried through the door of the busy coffee shop and he waved to Claire with a smile. Cameron, a tall, thin, well-dressed young man with short brown hair and intense blue eyes, carried a black leather briefcase and joined Claire at a small table near the windows.

"I was surprised you didn't want to meet at the office," Cameron said after they ordered tea and muffins.

"I really wanted to keep the meeting confidential." Claire eyed her advisor. "You didn't tell anyone we were meeting, did you?"

"Absolutely not." Cam sat up straight. "I'm happy to keep our discussion quiet. Whatever you need, Claire. You know that."

Claire had been working with Cameron for over

a year to handle the weighty portfolio she'd inherited from her husband and they got along well. The young man was easy to talk to, listened to her concerns and investment ideas, and offered good advice about how to maintain and grow the assets.

"I brought along a folder with a summary of your investments." Cameron reached to unzip the briefcase.

"That's okay, Cam," Claire told him. "I'm interested in talking about something other than my portfolio."

Cameron looked at Claire with surprise, wondering what one of his most important clients had on her mind. "Oh." He folded his hands on the tabletop. "How can I help?"

Picking up the mug of tea that had been placed on the table by the server, Claire sipped and then let out a sigh. "You may or may not know, but I was the person who found the body of Ashley Smith, an associate at the firm, who was recently murdered behind the State House."

Cameron's facial expression didn't change, but his eyes locked onto Claire's and he swallowed hard. "I didn't know that you were the one who found Ashley," he said quietly. "I'm very sorry."

"I wanted to talk to you about her. Since I found

Ashley, well, I can't get the murder out of my mind. I wondered if you knew her or if you knew someone who knew her."

Cameron said, "I knew Ashley from the firm's meetings and social events. We were friendly, but not friends or anything like that. We've chatted. We've been at the same large charity events." He looked down at his hands. "It was a shock to hear about the murder. I really couldn't believe it. It was so unexpected that it hit hard." He made eye contact with Claire. "The fragility of life. I guess you're well acquainted with that," Cameron said making reference to Claire losing her husband, Teddy.

Claire gave a nod of understanding and said, "I met with Bradford Bilson recently."

A look of concern washed over Cameron's face for a moment and noticing it, Claire told him, "It had nothing to do with my accounts. I'm very happy working with you. Bilson got in touch with *me*. He asked if I would meet him in a private location. He knew I'd found Ashley's body. He wanted to talk to me about it."

"How did he know you found her?"

"I have no idea. Maybe he has contacts with the police?" Claire wondered aloud.

For a moment, Cameron didn't say anything

until he finally asked, "Why did Bilson want to talk to you about Ashley's murder?"

"That was my very question ... and I still don't know the answer. Somehow he knew I found the body. Maybe because he knows my association with the firm and because I found her, he wanted to know what I knew?"

"What did he ask you?"

"He asked about the circumstances of how I found Ashley. He wanted to know what was in the car, if she'd been robbed, the condition of the body. Things I thought were morbid. I didn't understand why he wanted to know those things. I gave him a cursory description of how I came upon the car. I didn't think it was appropriate to give any more information."

"That's understandable," Cameron agreed. "Did Bilson press you for more details?"

"I told him he should ask the police for the details and that stopped him from asking more questions like that."

"Why would he want to know those things?" Cameron asked.

"Bilson said it was out of concern for an employee," Claire said. "He also admitted he didn't want anything to reflect poorly on the firm."

Cameron rolled his eyes. "That's the kind of worry I would expect from him, not so much any concern for what happened to Ashley."

Claire asked, "Do you know anything about Ashley or her boyfriend, Michael Burton?"

"I know who Michael is, but like Ashley, I didn't have much to do with him. We handle different accounts, different clients. We work on different floors of the building." Cameron leaned forward. "I did hear that Ashley and Michael were in a relationship for a while, but then it seemed to have soured."

"You heard this from someone at the firm?"

"I did. I won't mention the person's name, if you don't mind."

"Okay, that's fine." Claire hoped Cameron might have more to say on the subject.

"I know someone who worked with Ashley, another client associate. She told me Ashley didn't seem herself for about a month before the murder. Ashley was distracted, easily irked, almost depressed at times, like something was really bothering her. She'd made a few mistakes that my friend caught and alerted her to. She told me it was very, very unlike Ashley to be that inattentive and short-tempered."

"Did your friend ask Ashley what was wrong?"

"Yes," Cameron said. "Ashley told her *everything* was wrong. My friend tried to get her to share her troubles, but Ashley wasn't having it. She wouldn't open up. My friend feels awful, like she let Ashley down, like she should have shown more concern, tried to get Ashley to talk."

Claire sucked in a breath and let it out slowly. "I doubt that would have prevented what happened. Did your friend have any ideas what might have been the cause of Ashley's distress?"

"My friend told me Ashley went to the doctor a couple of times during the month she was so upset. She never knew what the appointments were about though."

"Was there any indication of something like drug use?" Claire asked.

"No, nothing like that. Ashley didn't do drugs. She barely would have one glass of wine at the firm's events."

"Do you think she was working on a case that caused her distress? Did she find out that something illegal might have been going on?"

"My friend didn't mention anything like that." Cameron shook his head. "Their clients are all very straightforward cases. Everything is pretty ordinary with their client lists. More complicated portfolios would be handled by the experienced senior advisors." The young man's eyes widened. "I don't mean to imply that there's illegal activity going on at upper levels."

Claire smiled. "I know," she reassured him. "Did you or your friend ever see Ashley interact with Michael?"

Cameron blew out a breath. "Michael is immature. He's all about the ladies. Thinks every woman worships him. My wife can't stand the guy. She's seen him in action at the things we attend for the firm. He flirts, has his hands on women, even when he was living with Ashley he did this stuff, right in front of her. I don't know why she ever put up with it. Ashley was a beautiful woman, intelligent, well-educated, did her job well. She must have had plenty of guys who were interested in her. Why she chose Michael Burton, and put up with his behavior, is beyond me."

"I guess there's no way to explain who we fall for." Claire gave a wistful smile.

"Maybe Ashley attracted weirdos for some reason. You know that local cookbook guy?" Cameron asked. "The Boston guy who has all the restaurants?"

"I think I know who you mean," Claire said.

"Well, my wife and I attended a fundraiser in New York City for the New York arm of Pennington Wealth. Ashley and my friend were there, too. Anyway, the cookbook guy was hitting on Ashley all night long. He was a real pain. My wife wanted to punch him in the nose."

"Did something happen?" Claire's intuition started to ping.

"By the end of the night, the guy was all over Ashley. He grabbed her and pulled her into a hug and tried to kiss her. She raised her voice to him and pushed him away. She gave him a little punch in his throat, nothing that did any damage, but he got the message finally."

Claire's eyes widened.

"Ashley was very upset and left in a huff. My wife actually applauded her." Cameron looked sheepish about it. "The cookbook guy seemed embarrassed and super angry. He was clutching his throat and muttering. He swore and growled about how Ashley was a witch and...."

"And what?" Claire asked.

"It didn't mean anything at the time, but, now, under the circumstances...."

"What, Cam?"

“The guy said something like ‘one of these days, she’s going to get hers.’”

Claire and Cameron stared at each other.

“When did this happen?” Claire questioned.

Cam’s face paled. “About two weeks before Ashley got killed.”

6

Detective Ian Fuller entered the chocolate shop and smiled brightly when he saw Claire behind the counter slipping a tray of cookies and muffins into the case. When Claire met his gaze, the man's kind, brown eyes warmed her to the core and she returned his smile, happy to see him.

"You're back from your conference already?" Claire asked. "I thought it ran two more days."

"I was called back early because of the Smith murder. I drove back this afternoon. I just got in."

Claire said, "It's nice to see you, but I guess you're not here for a social visit."

"Well, I would have stopped by anyway, but I do want to talk to you and Nicole."

Robby walked by with a tray of coffee drinks he

was delivering to one of the tables by the window. He nodded at Ian and kidded, "What about me? These two girls get all the attention. Don't you want to talk to me, too?"

"Of course, I do." Ian chuckled. "But someone has to hold down the fort when I take Claire and Nicole away from their work."

Claire handed Ian the latte she made for him. "Want to sit?" She gestured to the table in the corner by the window that had just been vacated.

He nodded and took his drink with him while Claire called Nicole from the backroom. When the three had taken seats, Ian got down to business.

"I want to talk to both of you about what I learned this morning about Ashley Smith's murder." He looked at Claire and inquired about how she was doing since coming across the upsetting scene.

"I'm okay," she told him. "I'm glad you're back. I have some things to tell you, too, but why don't you share your news first."

The detective nodded. "Even though I can't share everything, there are some details about the case you need to hear." Although Ian kept his voice down, he glanced around at the customers to see if anyone might be paying attention to his conversation. "You've heard most of the basic stuff. Ashley Smith worked at the financial services firm. She moved to Boston from Rhode Island, attended MIT's Sloan school, got her MBA, worked briefly at another company for two years before moving to Pennington Private Wealth."

"She lived with her boyfriend," Nicole said. "He worked at the same firm.

Ian said, "They met there, started seeing each other, moved in together about four months ago."

"Is the boyfriend a suspect?" Claire questioned.

"He was, however, he went into work very early that morning and was in the office when the murder took place."

"So the woman was killed shortly before Claire found her?" Nicole asked.

"The medical examiner's timeline puts the death about thirty minutes to an hour before Claire came along. The death was narrowed to a certain window of time because Ashley was seen at a corner coffee shop that morning shortly before Claire found the body. Ashley skipped her usual run, she told her boyfriend she had a headache. After getting up and getting ready for work, she walked to the coffee shop for a takeout drink, got in the car, and drove the two blocks to where she was shot."

"Did she always take her car to work?" Claire

asked. "The building isn't that far away. Why not walk and avoid the traffic and the hassle of parking."

Ian said, "Ashley usually walked to work with her boyfriend. She had a meeting with a client in Weston that morning. That's why the car."

"The boyfriend was definitely at work when it happened? His alibi is solid?" Something picked at Claire about the details.

"Iron-clad." Ian took a swallow of his latte and then made eye contact with each of the young women. "Nothing was taken from the car. Ashley's purse was on the seat, but nothing was stolen from it. All credit cards and cash were untouched. Ashley was wearing diamond earrings and a Rolex watch, an expensive one. She still had them on when the police arrived."

Nicole's eyes widened. "Clearly it wasn't a robbery then."

"Might it have been a robbery, but the perpetrator was interrupted before he could take anything?" Claire wondered.

"There is a security camera on one of the buildings." Ian seemed to wince. "The camera captured the murder. The time and date mechanism is broken so it doesn't give us any information about the time the crime was committed. As I said, we were able to piece that together."

Ian paused for a moment. "The person can be seen from the back. A man wearing a baseball cap, jeans, a long-sleeve shirt. He waves for Ashley to stop and she does, probably thinking the man needs directions. He steps to the stopped car, leans in. There's a flash and Ashley slumps. He reaches inside the driver side window for a couple of seconds, then calmly walks away. He knew the camera was there. That's why he was careful to never face in that direction."

"Can you tell anything about this guy?" Nicole leaned forward. "Can you use the security film to identify him?"

"Very unlikely." Ian frowned. "He looks like a million other men, nothing distinguishes this guy from any other young man walking around the city."

Claire tilted her head in question. "Why did he reach inside the car after shooting Ashley?"

"I was just getting to that." Ian glanced around the shop again. "The guy removed a ring from the woman's hand. The boyfriend had given it to her. He said she always wore the ring."

"Why take the ring and nothing else?" Claire's forehead scrunched up. "Was it valuable?"

"It was worth about four hundred dollars, a tiny fraction of what the earrings and the watch were worth."

"Why would he do that?" Nicole asked. "Why just take the ring?"

Ian cleared his throat. "Often when a crime is committed for hire, the hit man takes something from the victim to prove the completed deed to the person who hired him."

Both Nicole's and Claire's mouths dropped open. Neither one said a word. They stared at Ian.

"A hit man?" Nicole nearly spat out the words.

"Someone put out a contract on her?" Claire couldn't believe it and even though she knew Ian wouldn't be able to answer, she asked anyway, "Why?"

"If we knew the reason, it would probably lead to the person who made the hire and then to the killer." Ian's shoulders drooped slightly. "Unfortunately, we don't have the answer."

"Why on earth would someone take out a contract on Ashley Smith?" Claire shook her head and then sat up. "The senior vice president of Pennington Private Wealth got in touch with me. I met him on his private yacht."

A look of surprise showed on the detective's face. "He contacted you? Why?"

"Somehow he knew that I was the one who discovered the body."

"What's the man's name?" Ian reached into his jacket pocket for a small notebook.

Alarm shot through Claire's body. "You can't let him know I told you this."

Ian looked across the table at her. "Why not?"

"I don't want him thinking I ran to the cops after we talked. Even though he didn't come right out and tell me not to speak to anyone about what we discussed, since we met on his yacht and not in his office, I'm pretty sure that was the message."

"I won't say a word." Ian had a pen poised over the notebook. "What's this man's name?"

Claire locked eyes with Ian. "You won't say a word?"

"I promise. You know you can trust me."

"Bradford Bilson, he's one of the senior vice presidents at Pennington Private Wealth Management."

"He contacted you out of the blue?"

"Yes, but he and I have met several times." Claire couldn't tell Ian that the firm managed her money. The Pennington company only managed millionaires ... or billionaires and she wasn't ready to reveal her association with the firm.

Ian blinked at Claire, but he didn't ask her how she knew a man who was involved with such a well-known and prestigious firm.

Claire said, "Bilson asked me about my finding Ashley. He claimed to be concerned about her. My take on it is that his real interest is due to worry that the death could bring bad publicity to the company. I wonder if he thinks someone within the firm had something to do with the murder, an employee ... or maybe, a client."

Ian scribbled some notes.

"Or maybe someone in a senior position," Claire added.

"This is good information." Ian looked at Claire. "Anything else you think was important?"

"That's all. I wish it was more."

Concern etched into Ian's forehead. "My reason for telling you about the possibility this is a contract killing is because I'd like both of you to stay out of it. I know your involvement with the last two things was of tremendous help, but...."

"But, what?" Nicole asked.

"These circumstances are out of the norm ... and, well, it could be very dangerous. I'm asking you not to get involved. Please stay on the sidelines on this one." He looked from one young woman to the other.

Nicole took a quick glance at Claire and then said softly, "We can't promise anything, Ian."

Ian was about to speak when Nicole cut him off. "We appreciate the difficult and questionable issues with the case, but Claire *found* the dead woman. They lived in the same neighborhood. You know we feel a duty to help."

"We don't yet know who or what we're dealing with." Ian's face was serious. "And this time, trying to help could get you both killed."

Claire silently agreed with Nicole. She couldn't promise to stay out of the investigation, because deep in her heart she knew she had to help find the person responsible for Ashley Smith's death.

7

Little rounds of custard flans sat on a serving platter in the middle of the counter at Tony's Market and Deli with a few early-morning customers gathered around to taste-test the dessert while Claire talked with Augustus in the back corner of the shop.

"I'm familiar with the Pennington firm and I know who Bilson is. We've met a few times at charitable events." Augustus sipped his tea. "How do you know him?"

"I met him through my late husband. They were acquainted through charity fundraisers." Claire could tell by the judge's facial expression and tone of voice that he wasn't particularly fond of the man. "Why don't you like Bilson?"

Augustus's scruffy, white eyebrow went up. "I didn't say I didn't like him."

"But I can tell that you don't."

A little smile played over the older man's face. "You are a very perceptive person."

"I've been known to have strong intuition." Claire grinned. Augustus didn't know anything about her special ability to sense things from people and it made her smile when he commented on her perceptive abilities. "So why don't you like Bilson? Are his business practices suspect?"

"No, not to my knowledge. That isn't the reason."

"Can you share the reason?" Claire asked. She understood Augustus was privy to confidential information both in his time as a State Supreme Court Justice and even now as a respected member of the community and he was often unable to divulge what he knew.

"I have no reason to suspect that Bilson is other than a law-abiding and conscientious head of the firm," Augustus announced. "The financial institution has a strong reputation in this country and abroad."

"But you don't care for the man," Claire observed again.

"I don't." A cloud settled on the judge's face.

"I've heard some things about Bilson that I don't like. At the firm, he is very careful to be above-board in his actions ... in his personal life, however, he may not be so concerned with what he does."

"That's cryptic," Claire said. "Can you be any more specific?"

Augustus rubbed his chin. "He may do questionable things to fill his bank account."

"Like what sort of things? Is that all you can say about it?"

"I'm afraid so."

"Could Bilson hire a hit man to get rid of someone?"

"I wouldn't put it past him, but that absolutely doesn't mean he had anything to do with Ms. Smith's murder. The man seems to be the sort of person who would do what's in his best interests and the heck with everyone else. There are often checks and balances within an institution that keep senior management on the straight and narrow. I wouldn't do business with the man outside of the management firm, but don't go off thinking Bilson is responsible for having Ms. Smith killed. A person may not give a hoot about misleading people and bilking them out of their money to make a fortune, but murder? That is a big leap for someone to make. A very big leap."

"But I shouldn't eliminate the possibility?"

"There are probably only a few people you should cross off your suspect list. Us, Tony, Nicole, Robby, Ian."

"That's not very encouraging," Claire told the judge.

"It can be a harsh world." Augustus lifted his cup. "Hope for the best, but prepare for the worst."

Claire let out a sigh. "You're right." She shifted her gaze to the front of the store where Tony was directing the taste-testing of the dessert. The Corgis sat on the floor beside the man listening to his every word.

"It's important to take this seriously," Tony told three customers who were filling out the voting cards. "Think about the taste, the texture. Choose carefully. This is important to Claire and Nicole. Nicole is trying to get attention for her chocolate shop. As a small business owner, I know how important this is for her, so please, take your job voting for the sweets seriously."

Claire smiled. "Nicole should hire Tony as her marketing manager."

Augustus let out a chuckle and looked at Tony

admiringly. "Some of our discussions require us to talk about the worst in people. That man at the front of the market is an example of the best of people."

Claire was going to agree with Augustus when he spoke before she could say anything.

"And the woman sitting across from me is also one of the best." Augustus lifted his tea cup to salute Claire and she got all misty-eyed.

Her throat tight, she managed to squeak out a thank you. "And I feel the same about you."

Tony came up to the small table and noticed the young woman's eyes glistening with tears. "Why is Claire crying?" He shifted his focus to Augustus with his fist on his hip. "Did you say something to upset her?"

Claire waved her hand in the air and swallowed. "Something got in my eye and made them water. That's all it is."

Tony scowled. "What were you two talking about?"

"How great you are." Claire laughed.

Tony harrumphed and returned to the front counter while Claire and Augustus shook their heads and smiled.

Claire's phone buzzed with a text. "It's Nicole.

She says to come to work early. There's someone there who wants to talk to me."

Augustus said, "If you are going to continue to look into this case, then a word of warning, as always ... keep up your guard, Claire. Don't let it down for an instant."

When Claire arrived at the chocolate shop, she saw a young woman in her early twenties with chin-length auburn hair sitting at a table sipping a drink looking around the empty place uncomfortably. She perked up when she saw Claire. "Are you Robby's friend?"

"I am." Claire went up to the young woman's table. "You must be the person who wants to talk? Nicole texted me that someone would like to speak with us."

As Nicole came out from the back room with a platter of cookies, the woman introduced herself to Claire. "I'm Sally Burton. I go to school with Robby. My stepbrother, Michael, dated Ashley."

Nicole and Claire sat down opposite Sally.

"Robby said I should come talk to you." The girl's big green eyes looked from one to the other and she clasped her hands together tightly in her lap.

"You'd met Ashley?" Claire asked.

Sally nodded. "Not a bunch. She worked a lot, I'm at school, I work part-time and then I do gigs at night."

Nicole smiled trying to put the young woman at ease. "Do you sing?"

"Yeah. I play piano and guitar, flute too."

"Impressive," Claire told her. "Robby can attest to the fact that I have no musical ability whatsoever so people like you are amazing to me."

Sally seemed to relax a little. "Anyone can learn to play."

"Your brother dated Ashley for about eight months?" Nicole asked.

"That's about right. They moved in together a little while ago."

"What did you think of Ashley?" Claire questioned.

"She seemed nice."

Claire didn't think anything of importance was going to come from the conversation. "Did you ever go out together? Have dinner with Ashley and your brother? Did you have a chance to spend any time with her?"

Sally ran her hand through her hair. "I feel awful. I didn't get together with them much at all, I'm always so busy. We did go out for drinks one night."

"You had a chance to talk then?" Claire looked hopeful.

"I don't know much about Ashley. She was nice to me that night when we went out. We talked about music, what I wanted to do after I graduated. She told me she was getting tired of her job, that it was too stressful, that I was lucky to have so much creative talent."

"How long ago did you meet up with Michael and Ashley?" Nicole asked.

"Not long ago, maybe a month?"

Claire asked, "Did Ashley and your brother seem happy together?"

Sally's eyes widened. "Michael didn't kill her. He was at work. People saw him there. No way he would do such a thing."

"No, no, that's not what I meant." Claire tried to soothe the young woman. "We know your brother was at work." The possibility of a hit man floated in her head which would mean that whoever set up the killing wouldn't have been present when Ashley was shot, but Claire didn't mention any of that. "We know people vouched for him being in the office. I only wondered if Michael and Ashley seemed like they were serious about one another."

"I don't know how serious they were. They seemed happy."

"How's your brother doing?" Nicole asked gently.

Sally's lip quivered. "He's not doing well at all. He gave his notice at the financial firm. He told me he'd had it with living in the city. He's planning to move to Maine."

"He quit his job?" Nicole was surprised.

Sally nodded. "I think he's being too hasty, but he didn't listen to me. He only gave the firm a month's notice. He's already selling his things."

Claire asked, "How long has he worked there?"

Sally's face scrunched up while she thought about it. "He started right after he graduated college. He's thirty now, so about eight years?"

"Has Michael ever expressed dissatisfaction with the firm?" Claire considered that he might have been tired of his job and Ashley's murder may have pushed him to do something he'd wanted to do for some time.

"Not to me. Never."

"Was your brother unhappy living in the city?"

Nicole wondered if the man wanted a more suburban or rural lifestyle.

"Michael always loved Boston."

Claire needed to ask how Michael was acting before the murder. "Before Ashley died, did your brother seem himself? Did he seem worried or like something was bothering him?"

"Like I said, I didn't see him much." Sally seemed apologetic about not being close to her sibling. "We were both busy a lot. I'm not sure if anything was wrong with him." A tear escaped from her eye and she brushed it away with a quick motion. "The whole thing is very upsetting. Why would someone shoot Ashley? Why did this happen? Do you think Michael is in danger? Is that why he's running away?"

Unfortunately, Claire didn't have an answer for that.

8

Claire and Nicole found the brownstone they were looking for on the edge of the Beacon Hill neighborhood. There was a rectangular sign with the words *Tag Sale Today – Third Floor* pushed into the small patch of lawn beside the steps that led up to the open, glossy black, front door. Even though they weren't there to buy, when Claire saw the number of people who were coming out carrying items, she wondered if there was anything left in the apartment.

The large two-bedroom place had high ceilings, beautiful woodwork, and huge windows that looked out over leafy trees. One big room served as the living and dining rooms and the kitchen had been remodeled with high-end finishes and appliances.

People swarmed over the items for sale which included just about everything in the place.

A tall, good-looking man around thirty with sandy-colored hair and wearing jeans with a white t-shirt walked around answering questions and taking payment for the things. He was quiet and business-like and his face appeared drawn and tired.

Nicole exchanged a look with Claire. The man was Michael Burton, Sally's stepbrother and the murdered woman's boyfriend. The crowd thinned and as Nicole pretended to browse, Claire approached the man.

"You must be Michael," she said. "I met your sister the other day."

Michael made eye contact with Claire, but didn't say anything.

"I'm Claire Rollins." She gave her condolences to the young man and then said quietly, "I was the one who found Ashley in the car."

Michael's mouth opened slightly and his eyes widened, and his body seemed to shiver for a moment. "Claire? Is that what you said your name is?"

Claire gave a nod and told the young man again how sorry she was.

"It must have been awful for you to find her like that." Michael's already pale face had lost every last bit of color. He rubbed the side of his jaw.

Claire said, "Sally mentioned you were selling off some things. My friend, Nicole, is looking for accessories for her apartment so we decided to come by. Actually, the real reason was because I felt the need to tell you how sorry I was."

"I appreciate it." Michael shifted nervously from foot to foot as if he didn't know what else to say.

Claire gestured to the apartment sale. "You're leaving town?"

"I can't stay here anymore."

"Where will you go?" Claire's voice held a kind tone.

"I have a little cottage up in Maine, way up in the woods. I'm going up there for a while." The man's jaw muscles twitched.

"I heard you work at Pennington Financial. You've given notice?"

"I did. I'm not sorry. I need a change."

"Because I found Ashley, it's always going through my mind. I can't seem to stop thinking about it." Claire watched Michael's face. "Do you have any idea who might have done this?"

Michael bit his lower lip and shook his head. "No. I have no idea at all. It must have been some ... troubled person. Ash was in the wrong place at the wrong time."

Claire knew the police must have told him that Ashley's ring had been removed and that it could indicate a hit man was responsible for her death. The police must have told Michael to keep it quiet. The man might be terrified that whoever put out a hit on his girlfriend might also send someone to kill him. He must be getting out of Boston to keep a low profile.

Another thought ran through Claire's mind and it made her shudder. What if Michael is the one who hired the killer and is getting out of town to try and save his skin?

"I want peace and quiet," Michael said. "I'm a wreck. I need to go somewhere I can try and regain my sanity."

Claire asked gently, "Was there anything going on at work that may have worried Ashley? Was she concerned about anything, or anyone?"

Michael sighed. "There's a lot of pressure in a firm like Pennington, the demands, the clients. You have to be a certain kind of person to handle it. Ash was able to keep things in perspective. She was ambitious and resilient. She didn't seem worried about anything."

"Could someone perceive her ambition as stepping on some people's toes? Might someone have felt threatened by Ashley?"

Michael thought it over. "So threatened, the person would kill her? I can't imagine such a thing."

Nicole came over to them and Claire introduced her.

"Did you find anything you like?" Michael asked. He seemed eager to change the subject to something other than Ashley.

Nicole said, "I love that leather chair, but it has a *sold* tag on it. The same with the side table lamps."

"Yeah, too bad," Michael said. "A few days ago, the woman in the penthouse had a tag sale and sold all her stuff. I think you would have liked her style."

A flutter of anxiety scuttled over Claire's skin. "Someone else in the building moved out?"

"Yeah. My lease is up at the end of the month anyway, but hers was still in force for five more months. She didn't care. When she heard about Ashley, she decided to get out."

"Were you friends with the woman?"

A quick smile showed on Michael's face and then disappeared. "I'd never even met her before the other day ... well, I saw her once in a while in the building, but I didn't know her. People kind of keep to themselves in this building."

Nicole said, "She acted awfully fast. She must have really been shaken by what happened."

"She told me she'd tired of city-living and Ashley's death was the catalyst to push her into action."

"So she's paying the lease for five more months, but is leaving anyway?" Nicole asked.

Michael said, "The woman gives me the impression she has money. I guess it's not an issue for her."

"What's the woman's name?" Claire asked.

"Rose Smith."

"Smith?" Claire's heart skipped a beat. "The same last name as Ashley. They weren't related?"

Michael shook his head. "No. Smith is the most common last name in America."

"Is she still living in the building?" Claire's words tumbled out. "Did she move away already? Is she upstairs?"

"She left. She told me she's staying with someone in the Back Bay until she finishes sorting everything out."

"Why?" Adrenaline poured through Claire's veins. "Why not stay here in her own place?"

"I have no idea." Michael shrugged.

"Do you know where she's staying? Do you have her contact information?"

Nicole eyed her friend wondering why Claire seemed so shook.

Michael said, "Sorry. I don't have any contact for her."

Claire questioned, "Do you know what she did for work?"

"She told me she owned some clothing boutiques in the city. I think she said there's another one in Cambridge."

"Do you recall the name of the stores?" Claire tried to calm her tone.

Michael ran his hand over the top of his head. "Ah, it was something like ... oh, I know, it was *Rose in Bloom*. That was it." The man looked at Claire. "Do you think you know her?"

"No," Claire said and then made up a story. "I know someone who's looking for a short term lease. I wondered if Rose might be interested in subletting. Is she our age?"

"Maybe thirty, early thirties?"

"What does she look like?"

The man looked at Claire. "About your height. Slim, but has some curves. Long, dark hair, blue eyes. Attractive."

"Did Ashley know her?"

"Ash never mentioned her. Everybody's busy, working crazy hours. We never saw some of the people who live here, Rose included."

"Was Rose a client at Pennington, by any chance?" Claire questioned.

"I don't know." Michael's face registered surprise. "We don't know who all the firm's clients are. Why do you ask?"

Claire had no idea why she sensed something important about this woman. "Just wondering if Rose and Ashley knew each other."

More people had gathered in the apartment to look over the things for sale and an older woman approached Michael to ask him a few questions.

"Nice to meet you. Excuse me," he told Nicole and Claire as he went off to the kitchen with the woman to see what she wanted to buy.

Once outside, Nicole gave her friend the eye as they walked along the brick sidewalk in the sun. "What's going on? What are you thinking? Why so many questions about the woman who lived in the penthouse?"

"I got a strong sensation about her." A slight sheen of sweat showed over Claire's forehead. "My heart is racing."

"Do you want to go sit in the park? Rest for a while?" Nicole looked at her friend with concern.

"I'm okay. The feeling is strong. It's picking at me. Rose Smith. She and Ashley have the same last name."

"Smith?" Nicole rolled her eyes. "It's a pretty common name. How can that be important?"

"It is though. It's very important. I know it is." Claire stopped and turned around so she could look up to the top floor of the brownstone they'd just left. "Rose Smith sure took off fast after Ashley got shot."

Nicole's eyes narrowed. "Wait a minute. Are you thinking Rose killed Ashley?"

Claire met Nicole's gaze. "I don't know what to think. That's why we're going shopping."

"Shopping? Now? How is that going to help us figure things out?" Nicole looked at Claire like she'd lost her mind and then the reason dawned on her.

"Have you ever been to that boutique?" Claire asked. "*Rose in Bloom*?"

"Never," Nicole frowned. "I don't like shopping. I do everything online."

"Well, this afternoon you're going to shop the

old-fashioned way. In a real store." Claire smiled and linked her arm through Nicole's as they continued down the street. "And with any luck, we'll be able to have a little chat with Rose Smith."

9

The two young women walked along the street past the Boston Common and through the Public Garden to the Back Bay area of fashionable stores and restaurants. Claire had looked on her phone for the address of *Rose in Bloom* and they found the store just off Newbury Street.

The high-end boutique carried dresses, shirts, slacks, and swimsuits, cardigans, light jackets, and also had a small selection of expensive shoes and accessories. Cut-glass chandeliers hung from the ceilings, a grouping of white leather chairs were placed on one side of the room, the floors were light-colored wood, and the walls were painted a soft, creamy shade of off-white.

Nicole picked up a clutch purse, turned it over to see the price, and almost dropped the thing from shock. When she turned to Claire with a look that said, 'let's get out of here,' a tall, very slim salesperson with a blond bob approached with a cool smile.

"How can I help you?"

"We're just browsing," Claire informed the woman.

"For anything in particular?" The salesperson's long black eyelashes flicked up and down as she blinked.

Nicole wanted to say, *yes, for something we can afford.*

"Not really." Claire smiled and moved to a display table of necklaces and bracelets.

"Let me know if I can show you anything." The person sauntered away.

"Did you see these prices," Nicole whispered. "And there's something creepy about that woman. This is why I shop online."

Claire stifled a laugh. "Act like we belong here. Money is no object to us."

Nicole dramatically flipped her dark brown hair over her shoulder like she was a haughty celebrity.

Picking up a tiny two-piece swimsuit, she asked Claire, "Should I get this for our trip to the South of France?" She batted her eyelashes.

Claire stepped over to the saleswoman. "Is Rose Smith in today?"

The saleswoman's eyebrows raised a little. "Is there something I can answer for you?"

"I found out today that Ms. Smith is vacating her penthouse apartment on Beacon Hill. I'd like to speak with her about it."

"I don't think she's expected in today." The blond woman answered evenly.

"Is she at one of the other stores?" Claire asked.

The woman glanced around to see where the other employee was. "I'm not sure of Ms. Smith's schedule."

"Is there some way to find out?" Claire smiled.

The questions were outside of the script that the salesperson was accustomed to and she flustered a little. "Well ... I'm not sure. Jackie, do you know when Ms. Smith will be in?"

Jackie was helping a wealthy-looking woman choose a dress. "I think on Monday."

"Do you know if she's at one of the other stores today?"

"I'm not sure. You can call them and ask," Jackie said.

"Would you like me to call?" the woman asked Claire.

"Would you please? It would be very helpful."

The saleswoman nodded and clicked away on her high heels to the desk where she lifted the phone and placed two calls. She spoke for a longer time on the last call and every now and then, she would flick her eyes to Claire as she was conversing. After a minute, she rested the phone in its cradle and came around from behind the desk.

"I'm very sorry, but Ms. Smith isn't at any of the shops today. If you'd like to leave your name and a number, I'd be happy to give that to her when she comes in next week."

"Thank you, but I'll drop in again early in the week," Claire said with a pleasant smile and returned to browsing the store. When Nicole walked over, Claire whispered, "Ask the woman to help you with something for a few minutes."

Nicole gave her friend a look and then went to the salesperson to ask about a few dresses. While they were busy, Claire sidled over to the section of the store near the desk. She pretended to drop something, stepped to the corner of the desk, glanced around the top of it, and stepped back before anyone noticed her.

Checking her watch, she said to Nicole, "It's getting late. We need to be going."

A moment of confusion passed over Nicole's face, but she caught on in an instant, and told the salesperson, "I'll have to come back another day. Thank you for your help."

The two left the boutique and once outside on the sidewalk, Nicole asked what was going on.

Claire's eyes twinkled. "I watched to see how many stores the salesperson called. She spent more time on the phone during the last call she made and kept looking over at me. It made me think she was talking to Rose Smith. I took a quick peek at the desk for a list of their stores and the paper was taped to the wall right above the phone. I counted down the list to the second store. The street addresses were right next to the phone numbers on the list."

"Very clever." Nicole was impressed with the sleuthing.

"I suspect that Rose is at another one of her shops," Claire said, "and that she doesn't want to talk to us. Let's go see."

~

After arriving at the *Rose in Bloom* boutique in a heavily-traveled tourist section of Boston, Claire and Nicole went through the same questions and answers that they had in the first shop ... all with the same results. They slunk out of the store disheartened, crossed the street, and walked to a bench in a small park across from the building they'd just visited to discuss what to do next.

Claire tapped at her phone doing an internet search. "Here's a picture of Rose Smith."

Nicole took the phone. "She's nice looking. Sort of resembles me with the long dark hair, similar build, close in age." She passed the phone back. "If she and I are so much alike, how come I don't have her money?"

Smiling, Claire said, "Maybe someday you will when you expand the chocolate shop."

"Somehow I don't think so." Nicole slipped on her sunglasses.

A sudden gust of hot wind blew in the girls' faces and Claire's hair swirled across her face. She turned her head and pushed the strands back and when she did, her gaze shifted upward.

In one of the third floor windows of the building that housed *Rose in Bloom*, Claire spied someone staring out the window in their direction. Moving her position on the bench so it seemed she'd adjusted to better see Nicole, Claire kept her face forward, but her eyes focused on the person in the window.

"Don't look when I tell you this," Claire said, "but there's a woman in an upper floor window who seems to be watching us."

Nicole started to turn, but caught herself. "Which building?"

"The one we just left."

"Is it Rose Smith?" Nicole asked.

"I wouldn't be surprised."

"Can you still see her?" Nicole was dying to take a peek.

"Yes. She's still there."

"Checking us out?" Nicole asked. "Wondering who the people are who want to speak to her?"

"I bet." Claire kept the woman in her peripheral vision.

"It's kind of weird, isn't it?" Nicole made a face. "Why hide from us? Why not come down and have a brief conversation? What's the big deal?"

"I get the feeling that this woman is an important clue to what happened to Ashley."

"Is she the killer?" Nicole's shoulders shrunk

down involuntarily as if she was trying to make herself less of a target.

"I don't know. I'd love to meet her so I could shake her hand and try to pick up on what she's giving off." Claire took a look down the street. "There's an outdoor café a half a block away. Want to go sit there? We can watch for a while to see if Rose leaves the building."

"Yes, let's go. Rose staring at us from up there in the window is creeping me out." Nicole stood. "I'm starving. I can get something to eat at the café. And besides, I much prefer being the one who watches than being the one watched."

Claire laughed and the two headed down the street to the café where Nicole ordered a sandwich and Claire got a bowl of soup.

After eating half of her meal, Nicole said, "Let's think about Rose and the details we know about the case."

Keeping her eyes on the front of the building, Claire lifted her spoon to her mouth and then set it down. "Ashley was killed in her car not far from her apartment. The police think it was a job done by a hit man because Ashley's ring is missing, but extremely valuable things weren't stolen."

Nicole added to what they knew. "Rose and

Ashley had the same last name and lived in the same building. Right after Ashley was killed, Rose sold off her stuff and left her penthouse. Her lease isn't up, but it doesn't seem to matter to her that she has to pay for a place she isn't living in."

"Why would she do that?" Claire's eyes narrowed.

"She might have been scared out of her wits by Ashley's murder, didn't feel safe anymore, and wanted to get out of the neighborhood."

Claire said, "Or she could have had the move planned long before Ashley was killed."

Nicole looked skeptical at the suggestion. "How about this ... Rose has an idea who might have murdered Ashley and is afraid the same person will kill her."

"Clever," Claire told her friend. "Then would the women have known each other?"

"Not necessarily." Nicole ate a french fry. "Maybe they had a mutual friend or acquaintance so Rose knows something about Ashley."

"Take the sandwich with you," Claire said in a hurry as she tossed more money than was needed to pay the bill on the table. "I think our prey has just left the building. Time to see if we can follow someone without being detected."

Nicole wrapped her sandwich in a paper napkin and stuffed it into her bag, then she stood and winked at Claire. "Two amateur sleuths are about to practice a new skill. Hopefully, with success." She flipped her bag over her shoulder and she and Claire took off down the steamy, Boston sidewalk.

10

Claire and Nicole followed Rose Smith to a hair salon a few blocks away. It would be impossible to go inside and not be seen so they crossed the street and stood on a busy corner for over an hour and a half waiting for the woman to come out.

"What is she doing in there?" Nicole fussed. "How long does it take to get a haircut?"

As soon as the words were out of Nicole's mouth, a woman wearing huge sunglasses stepped out of the salon and Claire straightened up when she noticed her. "It's her, it's Rose."

"It's not her. Rose has long, brown hair." Nicole pushed off the brick building she'd been leaning against and stared across the street. "Wait. She went blond?"

A cab pulled to the curb and Rose opened the door and hurried inside. In a moment, the taxi sped off up the street.

With narrowed eyes, Nicole turned to Claire. "She went blond?"

"She cut her hair shorter, too." Claire watched the cab retreating into the distance. "It's chin-length now."

"She just had some urge?" Nicole asked with a tone of suspicion. "She's making a lot of changes recently, isn't she?"

Claire ticked off those changes. "She sold her stuff, left her penthouse apartment, cut and colored her hair. It makes me think she's trying to hide from something."

"Or *someone*." Nicole's face was serious. "This woman is either a suspect in Ashley's death or is terrified of something."

The young women headed back along the busy sidewalk in the direction of the boutique.

"Is she terrified of getting killed?" Claire suggested.

"What's the connection between Ashley and Rose? We need to talk to Rose and find out what's going on."

"I have an idea." Claire turned her head to her

friend. "Rose has gone off somewhere so why don't we go back to the building that houses her boutique? The building she was staring at us from. My bet is Rose is staying up there on the third floor. Maybe she has an office suite above her shop. Maybe she's staying there for the time being."

"Smart. Let's go snoop around."

When they arrived at the building, Claire and Nicole saw a ground-level, polished green door they suspected must lead directly to the upper floors. It was locked so they waited until someone came out and held the door for them.

A carved wooden staircase stood in the center of a small, tasteful lobby that had black and white tile flooring and a large ornate, crystal chandelier overhead. An elevator was located on the left side of the space.

"Walk up or ride?" Nicole asked.

"Let's walk."

Once on the third floor, Claire tried to get her bearings to figure out which side faced the street. They wandered the halls for a few minutes passing an accountant's office, a law office, and a dentist until they sorted it out.

"It's all businesses on this floor, nothing seems to

be residential." Claire spoke softly. "The room Rose was in has to be along this side of the hall."

A rectangular, brass plate on a solid door in the middle of the hall had – R. Smith – engraved on it. Claire smiled and knocked. They waited, but no one answered.

The next door had long glass panels on either side and the name of an attorney was etched into one of them. Claire entered with Nicole following behind and she approached the receptionist's desk with a friendly smile.

"Good afternoon," Claire said. "We wondered if you might be able to help us." She gestured to the left. "Does the next door office belong to Rose Smith? From *Rose in Bloom* downstairs? We wanted to drop in to speak with her and she doesn't seem to be in. We wanted to be sure we had the right place."

The twenty-something receptionist's light brown hair was cut short in a pixie style and her eyes were a bright blue. The name plate on the desk said, *Abby Wilcox*. "Yes, you have the right office. That's where Rose works. I haven't seen her today."

Claire nodded towards Nicole. "Nicole is a designer. We wanted to talk to Rose about carrying her line."

"Oohh." The girl looked excited. "I love fashion. I love to browse in Rose's shop."

"Are you friendly with Rose?" Claire asked.

"She's nice. A few mornings a week, she drops off coffee for me, our paralegal, and the attorney. We chat sometimes when we run into each other."

"She has a number of stores in the area, is that correct?" Claire asked.

"Four." The girl seemed proud of how many boutiques Rose owned.

"Is Rose usually in the office every day?" Nicole questioned.

"Usually." The young woman nodded. "Though this week she's been coming and going. Rose must be super busy. She hasn't brought us coffee this week. She usually keeps her door open when she's in the office, but it's been closed every day this week."

"Does she have a partner?"

The young woman asked, "In business, do you mean, or like a boyfriend?"

Nicole said, "Both."

"Well, she isn't seeing anyone now. She's been separated from her husband for quite a while. She had a business partner for several months, but now she's on her own again. He hasn't been around."

"How long ago did she break off with the partner?" Claire asked.

"Hmm, maybe a month or so?" The girl gave a shrug. "I can't say for sure."

"Do you know the partner's name?"

"It was Melvin." She rolled her eyes. "Melvin Watts. He wasn't the most pleasant person."

"No?" Nicole asked.

"He worked in the office with Rose. Sometimes I could hear them arguing."

"What did they argue about?" Claire questioned.

"It was hard to hear the words through the wall, but it was definitely angry voices. I didn't like it when we had a client waiting here. I'd turn the music up to block out the fighting." The receptionist took a look to the hall and lowered her voice. "Attorney Milliken went over there one day to ask them to keep it down. He looked angry when he came back. I asked if everything was okay and he just grunted."

"Was the arguing something new or did it always go on?" Claire asked.

"It was new. It went on for about a month before Melvin disappeared."

"If they weren't getting along, then maybe it was for the best that they ended their partnership,"

Claire said. "I guess we'll head out. Thanks for your time."

Heading into the hallway, they passed Rose's office and walked by the elevator when the doors opened and a blond woman with chin-length hair, around thirty, stepped out. She spotted Nicole and Claire, turned quickly to get back inside the elevator, but the doors closed before she could manage to enter.

"Rose?" Claire took a step forward. "Rose Smith?"

The woman froze and then slowly swiveled towards Claire and Nicole. With an expressionless face, she stared at them through the dark lenses of her sunglasses.

"Do you have a minute to talk?"

"Who are you?" Rose's voice was not friendly ... it held a tone of annoyance and impatience.

"I'm Claire Rollins and this is Nicole Summers." Claire hoped to be invited into the woman's office. "Someone told us you've moved out of your brownstone apartment on Beacon Hill and we wondered if you'd be interested in subletting."

"I'm not." Rose removed a key from her jacket pocket and headed off towards her office.

As the newly-blond woman slid the key into the lock, Claire asked, "Did you know Ashley Smith?"

Rose stood like a statue for several seconds, and then she quickly turned the key and pushed the door open. "No," she said as she slipped into her office.

Claire wanted to ask another question, but the door slammed and she heard the lock click. Looking back to make eye contact with Nicole, she said, "I guess that means she doesn't want to talk to us."

The corner of Nicole's mouth went up. "What gives you that idea?"

"She's important to this case." Claire's heart sank when Rose closed the door and locked herself in the office. Staring towards the room Rose had entered, Claire let out a long breath of air. "I'm going to try something."

Nicole's eyebrow raised as she watched Claire approach the office door.

Claire knocked gently. "Rose? I need to talk to you." She swallowed. "I'm the one who found Ashley Smith's body in the car and called the police." Hesitating for a moment, she went on. "My name is Claire Rollins. Nicole and I are trying to help figure out who did this ... and why." Claire leaned forward and put her ear close to the door, then she looked at Nicole and shook her head.

Nicole moved her hand in the air indicating for Claire to try again.

Claire thought about what she could say that would get Rose to open the door and speak with them. "We know you're afraid of something. In the few days since Ashley was killed, you've left your penthouse and changed your hair color and style. You're trying to hide. Are you worried someone is after you? Do you know who it might be? Maybe we can put our heads together and figure it out."

Not a sound came from the office. Claire waited a little longer, but nothing happened. Her shoulders slumped. "Nicole owns a chocolate shop in the North End. It's called *Chocolate Dreams*. We're both there just about every day. If you ever want to talk, call or come see us at the shop."

Defeated, the two young women left the building in silence and headed home.

11

As the sun set and darkness gathered, Claire and the Corgis snuggled together on the large sofa in the living room of Claire's townhouse apartment. The doors to the small garden were open and every now and then, a balmy breeze floated into the house making the woman and the dogs sleepy and lazy, only Claire wasn't able to doze because she couldn't stop thinking about Ashley Smith's murder.

She made mental notes about what she and Nicole should do next. Maybe they could find out who Ashley's friends were and talk to them. Maybe Ashley had confided in a friend about some worry she might not have revealed to her boyfriend.

Claire thought about ways to contact some of the woman's coworkers hoping that one of them knew something that had been troubling Ashley. Claire planned to call her financial advisor to ask if he could point her to some people who had known Ashley well.

Claire yawned. Her muscles were sore from running five miles in the morning and then biking fifteen miles with Ian in the afternoon. On the bike ride, she told him about visiting Ashley Smith's boyfriend at his apartment tag sale and the attempt to find Rose Smith and then finally locating her at her third floor office. "We couldn't get Rose to talk to us. It's pretty obvious that she's full of fear."

Ian reported that everyone in Ashley's building had been interviewed, including Rose, and law enforcement found no reason to suspect any of them, but when he heard Claire's information about how Rose had apparently abandoned her townhouse and changed her appearance, his face took on a serious expression. "I'll head over to Rose's shop tomorrow and talk to her again."

"Good luck with that," Claire told him. "The woman is elusive and uncooperative." She'd shared her impression that Rose was terrified and her hope that if Ian could get anything out of the woman, it might be very helpful to the case, and to Rose.

Lady snuggled closer to Claire so that her owner

could scratch behind her ears. Claire smiled at the pretty Corgi and ran her hand over the soft, multi-colored fur, while her mind worked on the different aspects of the case. After fifteen minutes of thinking and having her thoughts go around and around in circles, Claire swung her legs off the sofa and stood. She felt antsy and had the urge to get out of the house. “Do you two dogs want to go for a walk?”

Bear and Lady leapt from the couch and danced around until Claire was ready to go.

Grabbing the leashes, her phone, and the house key, Claire and the Corgis left the townhouse and stepped into the warm, summer night to stroll around the neighborhoods under the light of the streetlamps. Walking with the dogs as they stopped and sniffed at the curb, the bottom of light posts, and along the sidewalks, Claire’s mind relaxed and her ideas twirled less frantically. The tension in her neck and shoulders lessened as they ambled along the brick walkways and cobblestone streets.

Since the murder, Claire had avoided the street corner where she’d discovered Ashley Smith slumped over in her car, but tonight, she felt drawn to walk past the spot. Turning onto the deserted lane, the dogs, suddenly on high alert, stopped and sniffed the air. The fur around Bear’s neck stood up and he tugged on the leash wanting to dash up the street. The Corgis' behavior caused Claire's heart rate to increase.

"What's wrong, Bear?" she whispered. She looked up and down the quiet lane trying to locate the source of the dog's agitation.

The dog glanced up at her and then tugged on the leash pulling to move further up the road. Claire could see a pile of flowers on the curb next to the spot where Ashley's car had been parked, a spontaneous memorial for a young life that ended too soon.

The scuff of a shoe on the bricks caused Claire to hold her breath and halt.

A figure stepped out of the shadows. Claire gasped. The Corgis growled low in their throats.

The person facing them was the same height as Claire, slender, with a knitted hat pulled down around the face. Its hands were shoved into the pockets of a hoodie, the hood of the sweatshirt pulled up over the knitted cap.

A woman's voice said to Claire, "I wasn't expecting to run into you."

Narrowing her eyes, Claire tried to figure out who the person was and then it hit her. "Rose?"

"I came to add some flowers to the tribute." The

woman stood staring down at the mound of wilted blooms.

Claire was dumbfounded and didn't know what to say, afraid to spook the young woman and cause her to take off.

Rose glanced at the Corgis. "Your dogs?"

"Yeah," Claire said. The word came out soft and wispy.

Bear and Lady eyed Rose cautiously.

"It's okay, dogs," Rose told them. "I won't bite."

Claire swallowed her wariness, and worried that Rose would rush away, she asked the woman, "Do you know who killed Ashley?"

"No, I don't." Rose shook her head slowly.

"You've left your penthouse and changed your hair," Claire said. "You're afraid of something?"

Rose gave a little snort. "A lot of things."

"Does one of them have something to do with Ashley's murder?"

Rose didn't answer.

Someone turned onto the lane and headed towards them causing Rose to back away from the light of the streetlamp and move into the shadows. The woman's movement made Claire momentarily suspicious of the person coming down the opposite side of the sidewalk even though she was pretty sure it was only an innocent pedestrian.

Claire tensed until the person passed by.

She released a breath and looked to the shadows. "Does your worry have something to do with Ashley's murder?"

"It might," Rose said and stepped out from her hiding spot.

"Why?" Claire asked. "What do you know?"

"I don't know anything." Rose's voice cracked.

"You must know something." Claire wanted to hear any little thing, a tiny tidbit of information that could point her and law enforcement in the right direction. When Rose stayed quiet, she asked, "My friend is a Boston detective. Will you talk to him about your concerns?"

"Maybe ... if he can find me."

"Can he come to see you at the office above the shop?"

Rose blew out a long, sad sigh. "I won't be there." She tugged the side of the hoodie forward.

"Where are you going? Are you leaving the city?" Claire's heart dropped.

Rose said nothing.

"Please talk to me. What you know might bring Ashley's killer to justice."

Rose harrumphed. She looked up and down the street. "I need to go. I've been here too long."

"Wait," Claire almost shouted. "Can we go someplace to talk? Just for a little while. Wherever you want to go."

"No, I can't."

"Do you know *why* Ashley was killed?" Claire's voice shook.

"Keep out of it, Claire ... if you want to stay alive." Rose started away.

"Wait." Claire took a step forward. "Don't go. Please talk to me."

Claire's words sounded so forlorn that Rose paused. She opened her mouth, hesitated, and then said, "My legal name is *Ashley* Rose Smith. See if that helps you." She hurried up the sidewalk into the darkness.

Claire watched the woman rush away, not understanding how what Rose had just told her could be helpful. *Ashley Rose Smith ... Ashley Smith.*

The significance of the name hit Claire like a ton of bricks.

12

Claire called Ian right away and he came to her townhouse to hear the news.

"It was a case of mistaken identity." Ian groaned and ran his hand through his dark hair. "Two women with the same name lived in the same building. The hit man killed the wrong woman. Clearly, we're dealing with amateurs and either the person who contracted the killing was unclear about the victim or the gunman wasn't careful with the details ... or both."

One of the articles that came up when Claire did an internet search on Ashley Rose Smith was a list of common names in the United States and the website reported that the name *Ashley* was the first or second most common name for girls in the years when Rose and Ashley Smith would have been born.

Since Ian was on duty, he had to return to the station after discussing aspects of the revelation with Claire, and as soon as he left, she called Nicole.

"I'm still pretty shook up." Sitting outside at the table under the little white lights strung over the branches of the tree, Claire held out her hand to show Nicole how her fingers were trembling. "Can you believe it? The hit man killed the wrong person."

"I remember reading about something like this a few years ago." Nicole took a swallow of her coffee. "A woman hired a hit man to kill her husband, but the gunman shot the guy's brother instead."

"There are other cases like this?" A look of horror showed on Claire's face. "People hire hit men? Hit men kill the wrong person?"

Lady and Bear had been snoozing in the grass, but they both lifted their heads and whined. Lady walked over to sit at Claire's feet.

Nicole shrugged. "It's a nutty world and these hired killers probably aren't the brightest bulbs."

Shaking her head, Claire reached down to pat Lady. "I can't believe we're talking about things like this."

Nicole said, "So, it turns out we've been concentrating on the wrong person's life."

Claire gave her friend a puzzled look.

"Ashley Smith. She wasn't the target. We've been focusing on why someone would want *her* dead when the real question is, why would someone want *Rose* dead."

"Right." Claire rested her chin in her hand. "I asked Rose if she knew who killed Ashley. She said she didn't."

"You should have asked Rose if she knew who was *responsible* for Ashley's death? Who is the person who hired the killer?"

"Rose doesn't know there was a hit man, but she must suspect she was the real target. That information hasn't been in the news. Maybe the police are keeping it quiet." Claire leaned back in her chair and looked up at the night sky. "Why wouldn't Rose talk to the police? Why run off? She should tell the police what she knows or suspects."

"It's pretty obvious Rose suspects someone," Nicole said. "She took off from her apartment and changed her hair color. She told you her real name so Rose realizes that Ashley was killed by mistake, by someone actually looking for her. She must have an inkling who's behind it."

"The killing must have nothing to do with Pennington Private Wealth." Claire voiced her idea.

"Ashley and her boyfriend worked there, but Rose doesn't have anything to do with the place." She stared across the table. "Why did Bilson ask me to meet him on his yacht to talk about finding Ashley dead in her car?"

"It might have been out of genuine curiosity and concern about an employee? The general public doesn't know Ashley died in a case of mistaken identity. Bilson gathering information doesn't necessarily point to anything suspicious," Nicole said. "Of course, it doesn't hurt to keep Bilson and his motives in our sights. Maybe Bilson knows Rose. The man hasn't been cleared of guilt yet."

Claire's eyes widened. "What about the boyfriend? Ashley's boyfriend quit his job and is leaving town. That seems like guilty behavior. Is he behind the murder?"

A cloud settled over Nicole's expression. "Why would he hire a hit man to kill Rose?"

"That's the question that has to be answered. Who and why did someone want Rose dead. What about her former business partner? The receptionist in the office next to Rose's told us she heard arguing between Rose and her partner. What was his name? Milton?"

Nicole remembered. "Melvin. It was Melvin

Watts. What about someone who worked for Rose? An employee with a grudge?"

"When I was waiting for Ian, I looked Rose up on the internet. There isn't much out there about her, mostly articles and entries about her business, but I did find out that she'd been married. No kids. She and her husband have been separated for a couple of years."

"Interesting." Nicole tapped her index finger on the table. "Some bad blood between them? Money issues?"

Claire let out a sigh. "Too many possibilities. Where should we start?"

"We could go see Ashley's boyfriend again. Maybe he isn't getting out of town because he's guilty, maybe he's running away for the same reason Rose is running. He's afraid."

"But why would Rose and Michael be afraid? Why would both of them think they were in danger? They didn't know each other, they didn't work in the same place, and most likely, they didn't move in the same social circles."

"They had at least one thing in common." Nicole paused for effect. "They lived in the same building."

"My mind is blank," Claire said. "How could living in the same building be cause for concern?

And anyway, Rose knows it's a case of mistaken identity. She made that point by telling me her legal name."

"What if she's wrong?" Nicole looked pointedly at her friend.

Claire narrowed her eyes in question.

Nicole said, "What if Ashley was killed intentionally? What if Michael and Rose think they're next? Maybe they're all mixed up in the same thing. What if they *do* know each other and they aren't admitting it?"

"Ugh." Claire rubbed her temples. "My head is spinning. I'm getting a headache from all of this."

Nicole leaned forward. "Let's go talk to Michael, if he hasn't taken off yet. You didn't shake hands with him or Rose. You need to shake hands with him. See if you can pick up on anything from holding his hand."

Claire shook her head. "I'm not sensing much in this case. My intuition is weak."

"That's because you haven't touched any of these people. And, I don't think your skill is weak. You went out for a walk this evening. You said you felt antsy. You haven't been by the murder scene since it happened, but tonight you had the urge to walk past there. Your skill must have picked up that Rose was in the neighborhood. That's why you had the pull to go to the scene."

Claire looked at Nicole with wide eyes. "Huh."

"Your conversational skills are impressive," Nicole deadpanned.

The corner of Claire's mouth turned up at Nicole's comment. "I hadn't thought about why I had the feeling to walk over to that street. You could be right."

"And that would mean that your ability to sense things is improving, not diminishing. You must have sensed that Rose was nearby. You picked up on what was floating on the air, not by actually touching someone." Nicole gave a nod. "This is a good sign."

Lady rubbed her head against Claire's leg and Bear let out a little woof.

"See." Nicole smiled. "The dogs agree." Standing up, she said, "Let's go see Michael Burton."

"Now? It's late."

"It's not that late ... and if we wait, he might be long gone."

The Corgis jumped to their feet and nudged Claire with their noses.

"Okay," Claire joked. "I guess majority rules. Let's go see if he's at home."

With the dogs on leashes, Nicole and Claire

walked along the sidewalks to the edge of the Adamsburg Square neighborhood discussing the case and its strange twists and turns. The heat of the day had dissipated and the air held a slight chill causing goosebumps to form over Claire's bare arms. A breeze had kicked up and it rustled the leaves of the trees overhead.

"We've been so distracted by the goings-on," Nicole said, "we haven't decided on the dessert for our entry in the food festival."

Claire gave her opinion. "I think we should go with the custard flans with the Florentine cookies stuck into the tops."

"Stuck? I think we should come up with a better word than 'stuck' for the description of our entry."

With a grin, Claire suggested, "How about 'poked' ... or 'jammed' ... or 'shoved?'"

Nicole let out a chuckle. "Stop. I'll come up with the description on my own. You just help me make them."

"Why don't we make some sample trays of the desserts, put them out in the shop and I'll take some to Tony's market. We can get some final comments so we're sure this is the winner."

"Good idea," Nicole agreed. "Let's get on it tomorrow."

When they turned the corner and approached Michael Burton's and Rose Smith's building, Claire slowed her pace. "I'm feeling anxious."

Lady whined.

"Let's just see how it goes. We'll shake hands with him, remind him we were at the tag sale, ask a few questions and see if he's amenable to talking."

"Okay." Claire's heart beat pounded and a cold shiver raced over her skin. She looked up to the third floor. The lights were on in Michael Burton's apartment and he had drawn the shades on all the windows facing the street.

Claire watched for a shadow to move behind them to indicate that the man was at home, but she didn't see any motion. "Maybe he went out."

"Come on." Nicole took her friend's arm and tugged. They crossed the empty street and headed up the steps to the brownstone. A metal panel was placed over a few of the bricks with four names and their corresponding call buttons. "Burton and Smith" had been written on one of the small pieces of white paper and inserted into the holder for the third floor apartment.

Claire noticed the name "A. R. Smith" for the fourth floor, penthouse entry. She took a deep breath and nodded for Nicole to press the button.

When she pressed, the intercom let out a buzzing squawk.

No one answered. Nicole pressed again with the same result. “He mustn’t be at home,” she moaned.

When she looked at the door, Claire’s heart started to race and her stomach felt like it was filling with ice water. “The door’s open.”

The front door had not been shut properly. Nicole took hold of the knob and pushed the door wide so that Claire could enter first.

A low growl rumbled in Bear’s throat and the fur on Lady’s back stood up.

Nicole glanced at the Corgis and then to Claire. When she saw her friend’s expression, Nicole’s eyes went wide. “What’s wrong?” she whispered.

Her face pale and her jaw tense, Claire wouldn’t budge from the steps.

13

Michael Burton thundered down the wide, ornate staircase into the small lobby wide-eyed and panicky. He stopped momentarily when he almost plowed into the two young women standing just inside the front door with the dogs. Bear and Lady growled at the man.

Recognition passed over his face, and said, "Go back outside." Michael took Claire and Nicole by the arms and herded them out to the sidewalk.

"What's happened?" Nicole asked. "What's wrong?"

Michael, his breathing fast and labored, led them across the street, pulled out his cell phone, and placed a "911" call telling the dispatcher of a possible intruder in his building.

When he disconnected from the call, he said, "I got home, went into my place. I fell asleep on the couch." Staring up to the fourth floor, he rubbed at the back of his neck. "I woke up from a loud noise coming from the apartment above me. You asked me at the tag sale about the woman who lives there, Rose Smith. I heard footsteps and another bang so I went up the stairs to her place to see if she was in there ... to see if she was okay. Her door was open, what's left of her stuff is trashed. I panicked. I ran down to the lobby."

"Did you see Rose in the apartment?" Claire's heart was in her throat.

Michael shook his head. "I didn't stay long enough to notice." He sank down to the sit on the sidewalk. "Someone must have broken in."

"The front door was ajar when we arrived," Nicole said. "That's how we got into the entryway."

Michael held his head in his hands. "I can't take much more."

It wasn't long before a police car pulled up in front of the building. Nicole waved the officers over and Michael repeated what he'd told the dispatcher. When he tried to stand, he wobbled and sank back to his seated position. Instinctively, Claire placed her hand on the man's shoulder to comfort him.

When Nicole noticed that Claire was touching Michael, she made eye contact with her friend silently reminding Claire to use her skills to sense something about him.

Claire gave a nod and focused.

With their hands on their holstered guns, the police officers made their way inside to investigate. After fifteen minutes, they returned. "There's evidence of a break-in. Nothing much is left in the apartment, but the dresser drawers and a desk have been gone through and flipped over. No indication of an altercation or of any injuries. Whoever lives there has obviously moved out or wasn't at home. No one is inside. Seems like a simple robbery."

Claire didn't think it was a simple robbery. She'd texted Ian to let him know what had happened and he arrived in an unmarked car shortly after the officers emerged from the townhouse. An investigative team pulled up a few minutes after Ian's arrival.

Ian spoke with the officers and then took Claire to the side. "Someone's looking for Rose or something she might have left in her apartment."

"Do you think they were in there when Michael went up to check on the noises?" Claire gave a shudder thinking of what might have happened if Michael had entered the place.

Ian said, "Probably. Burton must have scared them off. The officers said the door of the back exit is wide open. Whoever it was may have run down that way and out." Ian's eyes softened when he looked at Claire. "Why are you here?"

Ian's gaze sent a flutter of warmth through Claire's veins. "Nicole and I thought it would be helpful if we talked to Michael."

Ian gently placed his hand on Claire's forearm. "I'm worried about this one. It's too dangerous. I wish you and Nicole would keep away from it."

Claire was about to speak, but Ian went on, "I know you want to help and you've been instrumental in the last two cases, but...."

"But, what?" Claire asked.

"I can't tell you to butt out even though I'd like to." Ian looked deeply into Claire's eyes. "But, I don't want anything to happen to you." The detective blew out some air. "It's late, you're unarmed, we don't know what's going on. Rose Smith could be dangerous ... heck, Michael Burton could be dangerous. We just don't know enough." Ian's voice hitched. "It worries me that you and Nicole will walk into something you can't get out of."

The emotion on Ian's face filled Claire's heart. She wanted to say something, but wasn't sure if she was misinterpreting Ian's words to be more than concern for a friend.

"I can't stop a citizen from talking to people, but you need to be careful, vigilant, on guard. Don't take unnecessary chances. Don't trust anyone. If you must talk to people about this case, do it in public places. Get away if anything seems off. Listen to your intuition."

Claire gave Ian a little smile. "I think you've given me this speech before."

"I don't think you listen so I'm giving it again." Ian leveled his eyes at Claire. "Promise me you'll heed my advice."

A lump formed in Claire's throat from Ian's concern. "I promise."

"Detective Fuller." A member of the investigative team called to Ian from in front of the townhouse.

"I need to go." Ian started away. "Are we still on for the bike ride on Saturday?"

Claire gave a smile. "Bright and early. I'll meet you in front of Tony's market."

"Make sure you're there. Safe and sound." Before crossing over to meet the investigator, Ian looked back at her with a serious expression. "Keep your eyes open."

Ian's words of warning sent a chill over Claire's

skin. She took in a deep breath and returned to Nicole and Michael Burton who sat side by side on the sidewalk. The Corgis sat to the man's right watching him closely.

"How are you doing?" Claire asked.

"Okay, I guess." Michael ran his hand over the back of his neck.

Glancing at Nicole, Claire squatted next to the shaken young man. "Maybe you should stay at a friend's place tonight."

"I will. I don't want to be in the apartment right now."

"Have the police finished talking to you?"

"I think so."

"How about the three of us go get a coffee or something? There's an all-night place a few blocks from here."

Michael began to protest, but he ran out of gas after three words.

"Come on." Claire stood, extended her hand to the man, and helped him up. Holding Michael's hand, she picked up on sensations of fear, worry, anger, grief, and confusion. There was something else mixed in, but she couldn't sort it out.

When they reached the coffee shop, they got drinks and carried them out to one of the tables set up on the sidewalk. The dogs sat and watched the people coming and going from the neighborhood.

"Did the police say anything?" Claire questioned. "Did they think it was a robbery in progress?"

Michael's voice was flat and gave the impression of exhaustion. "They didn't say much, only that the guy got away through the back exit."

"They need more time to figure it out," Nicole suggested.

"It's been days since Ash got murdered." Michael's facial muscles drooped. "I don't think they'll ever figure it out."

Claire watched the man's face. Only a little while ago, he'd been a young executive with a bright future, plenty of money, living in a vibrant city, sharing his life with his girlfriend ... then it all crashed down around him. Although she'd never lost someone to the horror of violence, Claire was familiar with the feelings of life crumbling to bits before your eyes.

Nicole and Claire asked Michael questions about where he'd grown up, gone to school, and how he'd chosen his career just to fill the air with comforting chatter. They didn't think he knew that Ashley's killer targeted the wrong person and neither young woman planned to be the one who told him.

"Did Ashley ever mention Rose Smith?" Nicole asked. "Could she have known her at all? Maybe shopped at the boutiques?"

"It's possible, I suppose." Michael took a swallow of his coffee.

Claire asked the next question and watched Michael's face carefully. "Before Ashley died, had you or she ever felt in danger?"

Michael blinked and his mouth opened in an "O" shape. "Danger? No. Why would we have?"

"Had anyone ever threatened you or Ashley?"

"No." He gave a vigorous shake of the head.

"Were you happy together?" Nicole asked.

A fleeting expression darted over Michael's face. "Of course."

"No second thoughts about moving in together?" Claire asked.

Michael's lower lip trembled for an instant and he looked away. "I...."

Claire could feel the guilt pouring off the young man.

"Ashley was eager to get married." Michael shook his head slowly back and forth. "I wasn't. I wasn't ready for such a commitment. For the past two months, things were off between us. I think we would have broken up."

"Did Ashley know how you felt?" Nicole asked.

"Yeah. We'd had some heated discussions about it." Michael ran his hand over his face.

"Was there someone else Ashley might have been interested in? Since she knew you two were probably going to break off your relationship, do you think she was interested in someone else?"

"No. I don't know."

"How about you?" Claire kept her eyes on Michael to gauge his reaction. "Did you have interest in anyone else?"

"Me? No." Michael's voice was loud. He swallowed hard and shifted in his seat without making eye contact with Claire. "I better get going to my friend's place. It's late. I don't want to keep him waiting." He stood. "Thanks for helping." The man turned and took off down the sidewalk.

"Touched a nerve, did we?" Nicole surmised.

"I felt a jumble of feelings when I held Michael's hand. Seems like guilt might be the overriding emotion."

"You think because he was seeing someone?" Nicole asked.

"When I held his hand, I felt a strong sensation." Claire looked at Nicole. "I think Michael might have had a thing for someone else."

Nicole raised an eyebrow.

"I think Michael had a thing for Rose."

There was something else floating on the air left behind by Michael's sudden departure that Claire tried to decipher. Her instincts and intuition told her something she didn't understand ... it felt like Michael had made up the story of an intruder being in Rose's apartment.

But why would he?

14

Claire had placed the platter of mini custard flans, each one decorated with a Florentine cookie, on the counter at the front of Tony's market for the early morning customers to taste test and to make final comments and suggestions. Tony and Tessa stood with the people who were trying out the sweets, chatting and taking down remarks from them.

In her fifties, Tessa was a psychic who had been helping Claire learn about her abilities and no one in their circle of friends except Claire and Nicole knew that Tessa had certain paranormal skills. When Tony met Tessa for the first time, he was immediately smitten with the woman and the two had been spending lots of time together enjoying one another's company.

Claire carried a few of the custard desserts to Augustus and she sat down across from him.

"Perfect." The retired judge announced his favorable impression of the flan and the accompanying cookie. "You and Nicole will certainly win a prize at the festival."

"That would be nice," Claire said, "but a husband and wife team who own a Boston bakery win every year. Anyway, the real purpose of entering the contest is to bring attention to Nicole's chocolate shop. I think we did a nice job with the flans. It's just the right amount of chocolate swirl in the custard, it's not overwhelming, and there's not too little to make an impact, and they look pretty."

"And this cookie is the crown of the dessert." Augustus chewed and swallowed. "Delicate, but with a lovely flavor. You have a real winner here."

Claire thanked the judge for his help in determining the food festival entry. "With everything going on, we've been distracted from making the final choice. We finally decided last night."

Augustus looked up from his cup of tea. "You and Nicole were busy last night?"

Claire gave a little groan. "This case is a jumble of confusion. First, we were looking at Ashley Smith's life trying to figure out who might have wanted her dead. Then we find out it was probably mistaken identity and the real target was Rose Smith." Claire told the judge most of what happened the previous evening at the brownstone apartment.

"You get the impression that the young man, Michael Burton, may have been attracted to Rose?" Augustus asked.

"That's what Nicole and I think. Of course, Michael didn't come right out and say it. He seems full of guilt and sorrow over Ashley's death. He also seems to feel awful that he was about to break up with her."

"Could this young man be behind the murder?" the judge asked, one eyebrow lifting up.

"I don't know what to think." Claire spooned some custard into her mouth. "What motivation would there be? Why not just break off the relationship with Ashley if he wasn't interested in continuing it? It's not like there's anything monetary to gain."

"Be careful not to dismiss suspicion from the man too quickly," Augustus said with a tone of seriousness.

"Really?" Claire questioned. "How would Michael benefit? Why have Ashley killed?"

"Let's discuss a scenario." The judge set down his

cup. "Michael wants to break off with Ashley, but he hesitates to do so because she is furious about it. Perhaps he thinks she will attempt to derail his career. They work at the same place. Ashley could have made things difficult for him if she knew the right people at the firm. She could smear him on social media. She might have known something about the young man that he didn't want to get out. He wants to rid himself of Ashley and the problems she causes him, he becomes desperate."

Hanging on Augustus's every word, Claire leans forward. "So he hires a hit man?"

"Perhaps ... or he kills her himself."

"Maybe Michael shot Ashley and took her ring to make it look like a hired killing." Claire's eyes darted around the market as her mind raced.

"But he was seen at work that day," Augustus said.

Claire's eyes narrowed as she thought of something. "So hiring a hit man and being seen at work, takes care of two things. Ashley is killed and Michael has an alibi and by making it look like a hit man killed her, suspicion is deflected away from Michael. Wow." Claire's voice was soft as she pondered the idea.

"Most likely, this scenario is incorrect." Augustus

lifted his cup to his lips and sipped. "However, it is not out of the realm of possibility."

"I never would have thought of this."

"I think you would have." Augustus smiled at Claire. "You're in the middle of it. It takes time to sort through the information."

"You're a big help to me," Claire told the judge.

"What about me?" Tony came over to the table and pulled up a chair.

"You help me every day." Claire put a hand on the big man's shoulder. "We're talking about how Ashley Smith came to be killed." Looking to the front of the store, she asked, "Where's Tessa?"

"She had to get to work. She asked me to tell you she'll see you later." Tony reached down to pat the Corgis's ears. "What's the news on the murder of that poor young girl? It really gets to me. It happened only a few blocks from the neighborhood." He shook his head in disgust. "You need to be careful, Blondie."

Claire brought Tony up to date on the details of the case and listed all the suspects she and Nicole had thought of.

"Sheesh." Tony looked from Claire to Augustus. "Is there anyone this Rose woman knows who *isn't* on the list of possible killers?"

"Everyone has to be considered," Claire said. "I would have overlooked someone if Augustus hadn't pointed out a few things to me."

"The police better get this figured out." Tony thumped his hand on the table for emphasis. "There's a killer walking around here." His face softened when he looked at Claire. "You be careful, Blondie. Take a cab home if you're out after dark. Call me, anytime, and I'll come meet you and walk you home."

Lady let out a little woof.

"I'll be careful." Claire smiled at the store owner. "Thanks."

A customer entered the shop and Tony got up to wait on him.

"I need to find a friend of Ashley's," Claire told the judge. "See if someone close to her has any ideas, find out if she confided anything that would be helpful." Claire broke off two small pieces from one of the cookies and offered them to Bear and Lady. "I want to find Rose's husband, too. He's a restauranteur in Boston. I read about him online. He owns at least five restaurants. Very successful."

"There's Rose's business partner to find as well," Augustus said. "Talking with him could prove fruitful."

Claire rested her chin in her hand. "There's too much to do. Maybe the police will solve the case soon and then I can forget about everything except working with Nicole and exercising with Ian."

"Someone will be brought to justice eventually." Augustus pushed himself up from his seat. "I must run along."

"Where are you off to?" Claire cocked her head in question. "It's so early. You're leaving before me? I don't need to be at the chocolate shop for another forty minutes."

"I'm heading to Brookline to meet a former colleague for breakfast." Augustus headed for the door. "Keep me informed about your sleuthing."

Claire nodded and smiled and after finishing her tea, she went to the front of the small market to find Tony to ask if there was anything she could help with before heading to the chocolate shop. Tony assigned her to unload a carton of pasta boxes to the shelf.

While Claire was sitting on a stool stocking the shelves in a corner of the shop, a young woman in her late twenties with short, caramel-colored hair came into the store and glanced around.

From behind the deli counter, Tony asked if he could help.

The woman approached the counter and asked in a soft voice, "Is Claire Rollins here this morning?"

Claire froze.

Tony pointed. "Claire's doing some stocking for me."

The woman came around the end of the shelf just as Claire stood up.

"I'm Claire." She eyed the woman with some trepidation. "You're looking for me?"

The petite, slender woman stepped forward. "I'm Meg Milliken. Do you have time to talk?"

"Go ahead, Blondie," Tony called. "I'll finish that up."

"I only have a few minutes," Claire apologized. "I'm supposed to be at work soon."

"At the chocolate shop?" Meg asked. "I can walk with you. I'm heading to work that way myself."

Claire's eyebrow went up, surprised that the woman knew where she worked. "Okay, sure." She said goodbye to Tony and the Corgis and left the market with the woman wondering who this person was and why she wanted to talk with her.

"Sorry to bother." The woman walked beside Claire. "I'm a friend of Ashley Smith. *Was* a friend."

Claire's heart skipped a beat. She'd wanted to

find a friend of Ashley, and out of the blue, one shows up. It unnerved her.

Claire suggested they sit for a while in the park and talk.

MEG STARED across the green grass from their bench in the shade of a tall Beech tree on the Common. "There was a private service for Ashley a few days ago." The woman took a deep breath and went on. "I spoke to the stepsister of Ashley's boyfriend. She said she'd talked to you. She told me where you worked and that you were often at Tony's Market in the early mornings. Her friend, Robby, told her that."

Claire's heart started to race. She shifted on the bench to better see Meg and gave her an encouraging look for her to say more. "Why did you want to meet?"

"I'm uneasy about what happened to Ashley." The muscle in Meg's jaw trembled and she blinked fast several times, her eyes shiny with tears. "I'm afraid I might know someone involved with her murder."

Claire stopped breathing for a few seconds.

15

Claire's mouth dropped open and she almost toppled from the bench. "You ... you know something about Ashley's death?"

Meg wrung her hands in her lap. "I'm not sure, it's probably nothing, but it's been on my mind and well, I just need to talk to someone. At the service, Sally told me she'd spoken to you and that you were very nice and that you were the one who found Ashley and I ... I don't know." Tears spilled down her cheeks.

Claire put her hand on the woman's arm and mumbled some useless words in an effort to be comforting. "I know how upsetting it all is."

Meg patted at her cheeks and took a few deep breaths. "Sorry."

Claire said, "I've been asking around, talking to people, trying to figure out what happened to your friend. I feel the need to help find out who did this. I know someone on the police force and he always tells me to stay out of it."

Meg gave a little smile. "But, you don't?"

"I have a theory that sometimes people are more willing to talk to regular citizens than to the police. If I find out anything, I pass it along to law enforcement." Claire waited to see if Meg would tell about her worries without being asked.

The morning air was turning steamy and Claire was glad they were sitting in the shade as she watched men and women hurrying by on the sidewalks dressed in suits and dresses. Thoughts jumped around in her head while she waited for Meg to speak.

At last, the young woman said, "I'm feeling foolish. I think I've let my ideas get the best of me."

Claire feared that her talk of law enforcement and passing along information to them had thrown cold water on Meg's need to talk. "Tell me what you've been thinking. Small things can often blow a case wide open."

"I knew Ashley for about two years. I met her at a

charity thing we both attended. She was smart and fun. A nice person."

"Something happened that makes you suspicious of someone?" Claire asked.

"Not too long ago," Meg said, "we were at another charity event. Both of our firms like to have employee presence at the things they help sponsor, so I go. I should back up a little. Ashley had moved in with Michael, her boyfriend, a few months before we went to this event. She told me she wasn't sure it was going to work out. Michael had been growing distant. They'd been arguing."

"What about?"

"Ashley was ready to get married, she wanted to have a family someday soon. Michael felt differently. He had become moody, was staying out late a lot of nights."

"Was Ashley planning to end the relationship?" Claire asked.

Meg gave a nod. "I think that her breaking up with Michael was right around the corner. Ashley had enough. She knew there was no future with him and she wanted to move on."

Claire said, "From his behavior, it seems that Michael had lost interest in the relationship?"

Meg rolled her eyes. "He didn't like being with one woman. I think he would have been happy to stay with Ashley, but only with the condition he was able to see other women." Meg's eyes narrowed. "He told Ashley he didn't see anything wrong with a relationship like that and didn't understand why it would bother her."

"He wanted to stay with her then?"

"He said so. He told her he loved her, but needed to have an "open" relationship. Ashley wasn't on board with that idea."

"It seems that they were on different wavelengths," Claire said, "and wanted different things for the future. Michael thought he could change Ashley's mind?"

Meg straightened up on the bench. "I think there was a very important reason that Michael wanted to stay with Ashley."

Claire looked at the young woman.

"Ashley was loaded. She had lots of money, inherited it from her parents." Disgust washed over Meg's face. "Michael always persuaded Ashley to buy him expensive things ... clothes, electronics, vacations. She paid the townhouse rent, he didn't kick in a cent. She even bought Michael a car. I think he wanted her to stay around so he could benefit from her money. He'd talked to her about buying a condo at a ski resort and a place on the water in Florida."

Meg shook her head. "Then he could entertain his women at one of the homes while Ashley was here in Boston."

"Wow," Claire said under her breath.

"Yeah," Meg said. "Ashley knew what he was about. She would have given him the boot very soon." Letting out a sigh, she said, "Ashley told me Michael came up with the idea to take life insurance policies out on each other. In the event of either one's death, the surviving partner would receive a million dollars."

Claire almost jumped from her seat. "Did they arrange the policies? Had the policies been canceled?"

"I doubt it." Meg sighed. "You know how it is when you're in the middle of stuff, things you intend to do get pushed off. I don't know if Michael's policy on Ashley was still in force or not. Here's another gem. Michael wanted Ashley to name him in her will."

"What?" Claire couldn't believe the nerve of the guy. "Did she do it?"

"I'm not sure, but I know she wasn't sure it was a good idea." Meg turned to Claire. "So these are my reasons to worry that Michael Burton may have had something to do with Ashley's murder."

"The police must have found out about life insurance policies and whether or not Michael had been named in Ashley's will." Claire thought out loud.

"Can you ask your police friend about it?"

"He isn't allowed to tell details like that, but I'll let him know about it in case it's a clue they missed." Claire remembered something Meg said at the start of their conversation. "You mentioned a charity event you went to with Ashley. Was there something you wanted to say about that?"

"Oh, I got so caught up in talking about the financial aspects of Ashley and Michael's relationship, I forgot to go back to that. It's important, too." Meg squeezed the bridge of her nose. "I think Michael was seeing someone. On a regular basis. There were tons of people at this event. It was black-tie, fancy hors d'oeuvres, a band, complimentary drinks, ice sculptures, the whole nine yards. I ran into Ashley there, and Michael. Michael was off schmoozing with people. Ashley was furious with Michael."

Meg let out a sigh of disgust. "I'd seen him earlier in the night dancing with other women, having a really good time. He basically deserted Ashley and left her on her own. I stepped out onto the balcony to get some air and I saw Michael down below in the garden. He was engaged in a long, passionate kiss with someone. The woman pushed him away. Maybe she didn't want to be seen kissing in public." Meg's voice dripped with anger.

"You think he was seeing this woman behind Ashley's back?" Claire asked.

"I think Michael was seeing plenty of women behind Ashley's back."

"Did Ashley know what was going on?"

"She never mentioned it to me and I didn't think it was my business to bring it up." Meg shook her head. "I should have. I should have told her. It was all happening right under her nose."

"Was it a woman from work that you saw Michael kissing?" Claire asked.

"I'm not sure who she was." Meg's lips were tight. "I know Michael was after the woman who lived in their building. She looked a lot like Ashley. I had drinks with all of them one night at the apartment. Michael was practically drooling over this neighbor of theirs."

Rose. Claire's heart rate increased. "Did you tell the police what you've told me?"

"No." Meg's eyes looked sad. "The police didn't talk to me. I wanted to run this by someone first. When Michael's sister told me she'd talked to you, I decided to find you. What do you think about all of this? Do you think I should tell the police?"

Claire nodded. "Yes. Tell them. It could be very important."

Meg checked the time on her phone. "I need to get to work." After thanking Claire, Meg headed off down the path through the park to the financial district.

With the conversation replaying in her mind, Claire got up and walked towards the North End. Rose and Michael? Claire had sensed that Michael was attracted to Rose. Had they started a relationship?

She stopped in her tracks. Rose told Claire her real name. Was she attempting to switch the focus of the murder to throw off the police? To make it seem that Rose was really the intended victim and not Ashley? Were Rose and Michael working together? Did they plot Ashley's murder to get rid of her ... and to get access to some of her money?

Her thoughts were spinning so fast, Claire almost felt dizzy. She needed to talk it over with Nicole. *What is going on?*

16

Claire, Robby, and Nicole discussed what Ashley's friend had revealed about Michael Burton and his relationship with the murdered woman.

Robby was horrified. "His sister is so nice. How could Michael be such a conniving monster?"

"Siblings can be very different people from one another," Nicole pointed out as she ran the mixer in the back room of the chocolate shop. "And they're not blood siblings anyway. The information about Michael being so eager to get at Ashley's money, wanting to be able to see other women, and his possible relationship with Rose is all concerning. He had motive to kill Ashley. We need to move him to the top of the suspect list."

Giving Claire the eye, Robby asked, "What does Clairvoyant Claire think?"

Claire rolled her eyes. "The jury is still out." After sliding a tray of cookies into the oven, she'd said, "I think we need to find some people who know Rose. We need to find out more about her."

"We need to talk to her husband, too." Nicole spooned dough onto a baking sheet. "What's his name? Did you look him up?" she asked Claire.

"He's a Boston-area restauranteur. His name is Ricky Harris."

Nicole spun around, her eyes wide. "Ricky Harris? He's the organizer of the food festival."

"Well, then," Robby smiled. "You'll have plenty of time to talk to him at the all-day food contest."

"Okay," Claire said, shaking her head. "That's a strange coincidence. Now we know where to find him anyway." Adding some platters to the dishwasher, she asked, "Do either of you know anything about Ricky Harris? What he's like? Any background?"

Nicole said, "He's well-known in the food community and not just in the city, all over the country. I heard he was offered a television show, but declined. He's written a bunch of cookbooks, has the restaurants, gives classes, has a line of cookware. He's a celebrity."

Claire stopped what she was doing and blinked. "This must be the guy that Cameron, my financial advisor, told me about. Remember he told me that he, his wife, some people from Pennington Wealth, and Ashley were in New York City at a fundraiser sponsored by the firm? The cookbook person was all over Ashley trying to kiss her until she pushed him in the throat?"

Nicole nodded. "And the man muttered about how Ashley would get hers someday. Oh, gosh, it was Ricky Harris who was bothering her."

"Have you heard anything about his reputation?" Claire asked.

"I know he's pretty hard-driving, demanding," Nicole said. "He rubs some people the wrong way, but I suppose that's expected when someone has so much going on and has so many people to work with. You can't please everyone."

"He certainly didn't please Ashley," Robby noted.

"We'd better keep our eyes on him," Claire said. "Sounds like he's hard on his employees. Maybe he's something worse."

Nicole eyed Robby and Claire. "Hopefully, you two would only say nice things about me."

"Right," Robby deadpanned.

In the late afternoon, the chocolate shop threesome entered the *Rose in Bloom* boutique with the hope of talking to the employees about their boss. Robby went along because he told the young women he often shopped there with a friend and knew some of the staff.

Arriving at the boutique, Robby walked into the shop like he owned the place. "I love this store. My friend from school has a healthy budget, courtesy of his mom and dad, and is a regular here. I come along for the fun of it."

One of the chic, fifty-something, blond saleswomen greeted Robby with a wide smile. "Good afternoon, Robby. Where's Allen?"

"Hello, Liz. Nice to see you. Allen has a class. I'm browsing with my gal pals today." Robby started off to the menswear section of the store.

Claire's eyebrow raised at the sales staff's familiarity with the young man. She whispered, "You didn't tell us you were on a first name basis with the people working here."

"You didn't ask." Robby held a blue, striped shirt up to himself and looked in the mirror.

"Is Rose here when you usually come in?" Claire asked.

"I've never met her. I've only dealt with the salespeople."

When Liz came over to help Robby, Claire asked about Rose. "Is she working today?"

"Not today." The question had changed the woman's friendly expression to a tight, unpleasant one. She went to the rack to get two shirts for Robby to try on.

"Ask her about Rose," Claire told him and moved away.

When the salesperson came back, Claire pretended to busy herself with looking at the jewelry on a display table a few yards away. Nicole was chatting with the saleswoman behind the counter.

"Is Rose working in another store today?" Robby ran his hand over the fabric of one of the shirts. "I need to speak with her about a sponsorship for an event at school." Giving the saleswoman a grin, he said, "Guess what? The theme of the show is all about roses. I spoke with Rose briefly a couple of weeks ago about it and she was very interested. I haven't been able to contact her. Any ideas on how to reach her? I wouldn't want her to miss out on the opportunity."

Claire smiled to herself at Robby's cleverness and smooth manner.

Liz said, "You might need to forget about getting in touch with Rose. I don't think she'll be back in time to help out with a sponsorship."

"Where did she go?" Robby picked out two other shirts to try on.

"She's away," Liz said with an unfavorable tone.

"A new man?" Robby leaned close to Liz. "Off on a little rendezvous with him?"

"Not quite."

Robby made eye contact with Liz and smiled. "Someone's hiding what seems to be some very interesting information."

"It's not like that." Liz's cheeks tinged pink. "Rose told the staff via email that she needed to go away due to an emergency and would be gone for several weeks."

"Does each store have its own manager?" Robby asked.

"Yes, and an assistant manager, but.... Rose has caused some tension here in the store." Liz looked around to see if anyone was listening. "Rose approached the manager here, Beverly, about buying the stores. Beverly had made her interest known to Rose for a couple of years. She was thrilled when Rose stated that it might be time for her to sell. They started talks to negotiate a price and were close to an agreement."

"What happened?"

"A month ago, Rose pulled out of the deal. She said she'd changed her mind. Beverly was furious. She'd already sold her home in Newton planning to move to the city to run the boutiques. She also owned a small shop in Newton which she sold. She had the financing all arranged to buy Rose's shops. Then, Beverly found out Rose had another buyer who was willing to pay more. I've never seen anyone as angry as Beverly was when she found out she wasn't getting the *Rose in Bloom* stores."

"Could she sue Rose?" Robby questioned.

"The contract hadn't yet been signed, so no, I guess not."

"Did Beverly quit as manager?"

"She sure did. A few weeks ago. She said, 'Let Rose find some other sucker to run her lousy boutique.' She stormed out and hasn't been seen since. Now Rose has disappeared for a while and we have no manager to run things. It's a real mess."

Hearing Liz tell the story of trouble between Rose and Beverly caused the little hairs on Claire's arms to stand up. Could Beverly be so angry about losing the stores that she would kill over it? The timing seemed right. Did Beverly hire a hit man to kill Rose? Did the killer confuse the identities and end up shooting Ashley by mistake?

"Have you been in touch with Beverly?" Robby asked.

"I called her a few days ago to see how she was doing." Liz made a face. "Her phone number is no longer in service."

"Did Beverly move away?"

"No one knows. She was good friends with the woman working at the counter." Liz nodded to the back of the shop. "She hasn't been able to get in touch with Beverly either. She even went to the apartment Beverly had rented and no one is ever there. It's like she just up and disappeared."

"Do you know who Rose was planning to sell the shops to?"

"Her business partner, Melvin Watts," Liz grumped. "A bad choice, if you ask me. The guy starts off all friendly, nice, pleasant and then he turns rude and mean. He and Rose were often fighting. If he was the owner, he'd never be able to keep the employees happy. Everyone would quit."

"Why would Rose sell to Watts then?"

Liz rubbed her thumb, index finger, and middle

finger together in the gesture for *money*. "Because of the cash."

"Did the sale to him go through?"

"I don't think so. As far as we know, we still work for Rose." Liz smiled at Robby. "Why don't you and Allen buy the boutiques?"

Robby sighed. "My first love is music."

"Well," Liz kidded, "your second love could be running these shops."

Robby tried on the shirts, but said he didn't want to make a decision without his friend, Allen's, opinion. He, Claire, and Nicole thanked Liz for her help and left the boutique to stroll down Newbury Street.

When Nicole heard what Robby had learned about Rose and Beverly, she nodded her head. "The woman at the counter told me the same things, only not in so much detail. She's worried about Beverly. She can't imagine her friend would take off and move away without telling her. The store is in chaos with no one in charge."

Claire wondered aloud if Beverly could be behind the murder of Ashley Smith. "Beverly could have hired someone to kill Rose and the attacker made a stupid mistake."

"The suspect list gets longer and longer. There's a whole lot of anger and misfortune going around,"

Nicole said with a sigh. “So what’s next? We find Rose’s former business partner, Melvin Watts?”

“And we’ll talk to Rose’s husband at the food festival,” Claire said.

“I’d better come along when you talk to them.” Robby’s eyes twinkled. “You saw how my charming personality worked in the boutique.”

“Yeah, come with us,” Nicole said, “if things don’t go well, we’ll pin the blame on you.”

Charming. Blame. The words swirled through the air and picked and pulled at Claire sending a shiver over her skin.

17

Claire tracked down Melvin Watts at his office in Boston's Seaport district and she and Nicole paid the man a visit after the chocolate shop closed for the day. The office was on the ninth floor of a fancy, new, ten-story building with walls of windows offering a spectacular view of the harbor.

The reception room desk was occupied by a very attractive, efficient, young, blue-eyed, blonde dressed in a fitted business suit. The space had high ceilings, light gray walls, wood floors covered with expensive area rugs, and groupings of furniture in shades of subtle blues and grays.

"I wasn't expecting a place like this." Nicole admired the view of the ocean while they waited in the reception area. "I had no inkling Watts was so successful."

Claire's research on the company revealed that Watts Industries had holdings in strip malls, city buildings, and industrial parks.

"Why would Watts want anything to do with fashion boutiques?" Claire wondered aloud. "It doesn't seem to fit in with his business objectives."

"We're about to find out." Nicole nodded to the man entering the reception area from the hall.

A tall, trim man in his mid-thirties with dark brown hair and brown eyes walked towards the young women with a warm, friendly smile. He wore a slim-cut, navy blue suit, white shirt, and yellow tie. Watts had high cheekbones, perfect white teeth, wide-set eyes, and symmetrical features. Handsome and fit, he looked like he stepped from the pages of a fashion magazine.

"Hello," he extended his hand. "I'm Mel Watts."

Claire shook and introduced herself being careful to try and sense something from the handshake. Nicole shook hands and they followed Watts to his office which was a smaller version of the waiting room.

Watts stood with the young women at the window and pointed out different landmarks and took time to share some interesting historical facts about the area. He expressed how thrilled he was to get the office space when it became available and asked questions about Nicole and Claire's backgrounds. The man was likeable and charming.

Claire recalled how Liz at *Rose in Bloom* had described Watts – *he starts off all pleasant and charming and then turns mean.*

When they were seated in leather chairs in front of a fireplace, Claire said, "Thank you for agreeing to meet with us. We met Rose not too long ago. As I said on the phone, she mentioned that she was interested in selling her boutiques. Nicole owns a chocolate shop in the North End and I have some experience in business. After meeting Rose, we discussed the idea of buying the business from her." Claire told the fib to cover the real reason they wanted to talk about Rose. "We've been trying to reach her without success."

"Rose and I worked together for about a year. I was only working with her a few hours a week. I was interested in learning the ins and outs of a fashion boutique." Watts gave Claire and Nicole a warm smile. "I'm thinking of expanding in order to have different income streams. At present, I'm fully invested in real estate and commercial properties."

"Were you thinking of buying Rose's business or did you work with her as a learning experience?" Nicole asked.

"It started as a way to learn the business, but I became interested in making the purchase when Rose expressed interest in selling."

"It didn't go through?" Claire questioned.

"Things fell apart." Watts looked across the room for a moment, seemingly to gather his thoughts. "Our association worked well in the beginning, but over the months, things started to sour." It was clear that the man was choosing his words carefully. "Rose seemed amenable to my offer. She told me she had two other offers that she was considering. I didn't realize I was in competition with other buyers. It took me aback."

Watts looked at Claire and Nicole and leaned forward as if he was about to share a secret with them. "Rose's business was struggling financially. She'd made some unfortunate business decisions and needed an infusion of cash. I provided the money to keep the boutiques operating in exchange for a share of profits and a chance to work closely with Rose to learn the fashion business."

"Rose didn't accept your offer to purchase the boutiques?" Claire asked.

"I withdrew my offer."

Nicole held the man's eyes. "How did Rose react to that?"

"She wasn't pleased." Watts sat back and rested his elbow on the arm of the chair.

"When did this happen?"

"About a month ago. I withdrew the offer to buy the boutiques and also ended our working relationship. There was a clause in the contract that either one of us could end our partnership at any time."

"Did that upset Rose?"

"Yes, it did, and I was sorry to do it, but it wasn't profitable and there was no point in continuing the association in light of our disagreements." Watts folded his hands in his lap.

"Were you and Rose involved on a personal level?" Nicole questioned.

Watts blinked and his eyebrows raised. "Why, no, we weren't. It's my thinking that mixing the business and personal sides of life is often a mistake." After a few seconds, he asked, "Why do you ask?"

Claire watched the man's face for his reaction. "Someone suggested to us that you and Rose were more than business partners."

A muscle in Watts's cheek twitched and a tiny flash of anger registered on his face. "I'm afraid that someone is incorrect." He shifted in his chair. Some of his friendliness seemed to have evaporated.

"We've been concerned that we haven't been able to get in touch with Rose," Claire told the man.

"I haven't spoken to her since we finished up our business transactions." Watts adjusted the cuff of his shirt.

"We're worried about Rose on a personal level," Nicole said. "It seems she's told her employees that she won't be working due to an emergency of some kind. The staff seems to be unsure how to handle the stores in her absence. It seems quite sudden."

Watts's forehead scrunched together in thought.

Claire made eye contact with Watts. "How did Rose seem when you were with her most recently?"

"She seemed, ah ... well, we weren't exactly pleased with one another."

"Did she seem unusually worried or uneasy? Maybe distracted from the dealings she had with you?"

"Hmm. I really couldn't say."

"We understand your relationship was strained at the end of your partnership." Nicole straightened in her seat. "Outside of that, did Rose seem overly sensitive? Did her mind seem elsewhere? Was she concerned for her safety?"

"Her safety? Why would she be worried about her safety?" Although, Watts's voice was louder and had taken on a tone of authority, he appeared hesitant to make eye contact with either young woman sitting across from him.

"There is reason to believe that Rose might be in danger." Claire raised her own voice.

Watts scoffed. "Why on earth would Rose be in danger?"

"Have the police come here to speak with you?" Nicole asked.

"The police?" Watts had to keep himself from jumping out of his seat. "Why would the police come here?"

"Out of concern for Rose." Claire leveled her eyes at the man. "Do you know where Rose might be?"

"How would I know where she is?" A sheen of moisture showed on Watts's forehead. "The last time I saw her was a few weeks ago. We haven't been in touch since then."

"Do you have any idea why she might have left town?" Nicole questioned. "Was there any small thing she might have said to you to indicate she needed to leave?"

"No." A stern look came over Watts's face.

Seeing the man's discomfort, Claire decided it was time to ask the next question. "Did you see the news about the woman who was found shot and killed behind the State House not long ago?"

Watts blinked fast several times. "No, I didn't."

Claire didn't have to touch the man to know he was lying. "Her name was Ashley Smith. She looked very much like Rose. They were close in age. They even lived in the same building."

"I don't know anything about her. Why are you bringing her up?"

Claire didn't reply. "How did you meet Rose?"

Watts's tension seemed to lessen as he recalled where he and Rose had met. "I met Rose through social events in the city. I believe the first time we met was at a fundraising event for one of the hospitals in the area." He nodded. "Yes, it was a private food event held at the ballpark, by invitation only."

"A food event?" Nicole asked.

"To raise money. Rose's husband is a well-known chef, Ricky Harris. He owns several restaurants. He runs a lot of high-end events."

"Do you know her husband well?" Claire asked.

"I know him. Not well, but we're friendly when we meet at events."

"Ricky and Rose are separated?" Nicole asked.

"They are." He shook his head sadly. "They've been on again, off again for a few years. Who knows when they'll decide to make it final."

"Do they still get along? Is it a friendly split?"

Watts seemed to tense slightly. "It seems to be."

"Did Rose talk about Ricky to you?"

"Not often."

"When she did speak about him was her tone angry? Friendly? Was she still fond of him?"

Watts ran his hand over his jaw and then looked at his watch. "I really didn't pay attention. Why all these questions about Rose's relationships?"

Claire told him, "Like we said, we're very concerned about Rose's safety. We'd like to find her."

"I can't help you with that. I'm sorry."

Claire got the impression that he wasn't sorry at all.

"I'm afraid I have another meeting." Watts stood and shook hands with the two young women.

Claire and Nicole thanked him for his time and left the office.

After touching the man's hand, Claire was sure that Melvin Watts knew more than he was telling them.

18

Claire, Nicole, and Robby had worked late into the night baking and assembling the custards and the Florentine cookies for the food festival. Nicole pulled the rented van up to the building that had signs on it indicating where the food contest participants should unload.

Assistants waited for the deliveries by the doors with long pushcarts to transport the goods to refrigerators and countertops and contestants' names were printed on placards to show where each person or team could finish their preparations.

The room was abuzz with people hurrying to and fro as they stored their desserts until they were called to the contest area. Nicole had planned to have a food tent selling her desserts, but contestants weren't allowed to compete *and* sell their wares, so she had to scrap the plan.

"This is like one of those television food shows." Claire took in the sight of the huge room separated with counters, stoves, and refrigerators setup for each contest participant.

"The excitement is crackling over the air," Robby said eagerly as he watched the hustle and bustle.

The attendant in charge of Nicole's sweets maneuvered his pushcart through the hall to the kitchen set-up assigned to her and he parked the cart near the refrigerator for easy unloading. "Good luck," he said as he walked back to the entrance to help another contestant.

Nicole looked slightly pale and her eyes were huge. "I'm afraid," she whispered to her partners.

"It's okay," Claire smiled, surprised at her friend's reaction. "Your desserts are wonderful. Everyone will love them."

"What if I'm way out of my league? What if I make a fool of myself?" Nicole's hair was pulled up in a high ponytail and she fiddled nervously with the ends.

Robby chuckled. "You are definitely not out of your league. Your nerves are firing overtime. There's so much going on in here that you're letting yourself get overwhelmed. Stop looking around and think about what we have to do."

A man with a microphone stood on a small, circular stage in the middle of the space. He welcomed the contestants and reviewed the schedule for the day. For each category, thirty volunteers from the crowd of festival goers would be asked to act as citizen judges and would join the three, well-known Boston personalities who were the celebrity judges for the day.

The thirty-three people would sample the offerings and would then cast their votes for the best in each specialty. The judging would be blind, meaning there would be no indication who or from which shop the items were from.

The voting for the desserts would be at 1pm in the afternoon.

"That gives us plenty of time to assemble the entries." Claire took her friend's arm. "It also gives us plenty of time to walk around the festival for a while. We don't need to be back here for two hours."

"Good." Robby led the way out of the building. "Let's go enjoy ourselves and get away from the nervous energy in here."

The festival was in a full swing with crowds of people moving through the displays. Large white-

tents were set up around the area. A band played on the stage, brick walkways were lined with food vendors, chefs gave cooking demonstrations at small stations, and other booths sold cookware and accessories.

The smell of delicious food floated on the air. The day was picture-perfect with a bright blue sky, warm, but comfortable temperatures, and little to no humidity.

The threesome made their way to an artisan pizza truck where they placed their lunch orders and then carried the food to a table set under a tree.

A long string of cheese reached from Nicole's mouth to the slice of pizza in her hand. She chewed and closed her eyes for a few seconds. "This is the best pizza I've ever had. I thank my lucky stars I'm not entered in the pizza category. If this is one of the entries, I wouldn't stand a chance."

Robby and Claire agreed that it was one of the best they'd eaten and Robby got up to order two more slices.

"I haven't seen Ricky Harris around." Claire turned her head to check the crowd. "I hope he shows himself before we have to go inside to ready the desserts."

"I've been watching for him, too." Nicole finished

her slice and thought about getting another, but decided against it since her stomach felt nervous and she didn't want to get sick right before her category was called.

They were discussing the questions they wanted to ask the man about Rose, when Robby sat down with his pizza plate and said, "There's Mr. Festival-Organizer over there." He nodded to the booth across from where they were sitting.

"Ricky Harris?" Nicole looked from side to side until she spotted the man regaling a vendor with a story. Harris was about six feet, six inches tall with a head of longer auburn hair that touched his collar. He had strong features and a hearty laugh.

"How should we do this?" Claire asked, watching the man.

"I'll sit here. You two go over to the vendor and order something. Then strike up a conversation with Harris." Robby took a huge bite of his pizza slice.

"Why aren't you coming over with us?" Nicole asked.

"I'm busy," Robby mumbled as he chewed. "Besides, two attractive women will be all that's necessary. Go ahead, get a move on." He waved his hand at them to go over to where Harris was standing. "I'll supervise from here."

Nicole rolled her eyes at her sandy-haired employee and then she and Claire made their move. Harris gave them a wide smile when they came up next to him.

"Enjoying the festival?" Harris asked.

"We are." Claire checked her watch. "We're contestants in the dessert category. We still have an hour before we need to get ready." She introduced herself and Nicole.

"You're Ricky Harris, right?" Nicole knew full-well that was who stood before her. "You're one of the organizers of the event."

Harris beamed, pleased at being recognized. He asked about their dessert. "I'm not judging today so you can tell me about your entry." When the young women described the dessert, Harris put his hand on his stomach and moaned. "I'm drooling just thinking about it."

After a few more minutes of conversation related to food and recipes, Nicole asked, "You're married to the Boston boutique owner, Rose Smith, aren't you?"

Harris's eyes went wide and he seemed slightly uncomfortable for a second, but then recovered his bravado. "Yes, I am, but we're separated, have been for a couple of years." It seemed Harris wanted to make sure that Claire and Nicole knew he was single. "Sometimes, it's best for both parties to move on."

Claire and Nicole used the same story they'd told Melvin Watts – that they met Rose and were interested in making an offer for the boutiques.

"We haven't been able to get in touch with Rose." Nicole's face took on an expression of concern.

"We liked Rose," Claire added. "We hoped to get together, on a personal level. She doesn't answer our messages, never picks up when we call, doesn't reply to emails. We're worried about her."

Harris's brows knitted together. "That's odd."

"Do you know where Rose might be?" Nicole asked.

"Me? No, I'm afraid not. I can't help you."

"Do you and Rose keep in touch?" Claire questioned.

"Sometimes, not often." Harris ran his hand over his reddish hair and glanced around at the people walking by. He gave off a sense of nervousness when talking about Rose.

"We heard that Rose had multiple offers for her business."

"Did she?" Harris took a small step back.

"Nothing came of them though." Claire kept her eyes on Harris's face. "We also heard that Rose left town suddenly due to an emergency. Do you have any knowledge about that?"

"An emergency? No. Like I said, we aren't in touch much anymore."

Claire asked, "When you and Rose were married, did you work together on your two businesses?"

"We didn't." Harris shook his head. "We kept things separate." The man's eyes were like lasers on the young women. He bent slightly forward. "When did Rose leave town?"

"We aren't sure," Nicole said. "Recently, though."

"Who told you she'd left?"

"One of her employees."

"Did the person give any details? Where she went? What the emergency was about?"

"She didn't," Claire said sadly. "We hoped you might be able to help us get in touch with Rose."

"Sorry. I don't know anything."

Nicole said, "We met with Rose's former business partner the other day."

Harris frowned. "Mel Watts?"

"Yes." Nicole made eye contact with the man. "We got in touch with him. We wondered if he might have any information about Rose. Like I said, we're concerned about her. Could she be in any danger?"

"Danger?" Harris swallowed. "What kind of danger?"

Claire said, "We have no idea, but it seems strange that Rose would abandon her business and completely ignore our pre-offer to buy her out. Have the police talked to you?"

Harris's face seemed to lose its color. "Police? Why? For what reason? Why would they want to talk to me?"

"About Rose," Nicole told the man. "About what's going on with her."

"I don't know anything." Harris vigorously shook his head.

"Does Rose have a friend we could contact?" Claire asked.

"Ah, maybe you could talk to Beverly at the store." Harris started to walk away. "I need to see to some things. Good luck with your entry."

When the man had disappeared into the crowd, Claire turned to Nicole about the employee who was set to buy the boutiques before Rose backed out. "Somehow, I don't think Beverly is going to be able to help us."

Nicole gave her friend a look. "No, especially since Rose isn't her favorite person at the moment, and more importantly, Beverly seems to have left town in a rage."

Robby came over to them. "How did it go? Did you charm Mr. Harris into telling you anything?"

Claire sighed. "We didn't."

"Why is he so nervous talking about Rose?" Nicole raised an eyebrow. "A few times, I thought he was about to jump out of his skin."

"Are we suspicious of him?" Robby glanced into the crowd of people that Harris had disappeared into.

Claire said, "Right now, we're suspicious of everyone."

19

The votes had been tallied and the stage had been set up for the dessert category awards announcement with each of the twelve desserts displayed on its own, separate table. The bakers and assistants stood in a line along the back of the stage and the four festival organizers, including Ricky Harris, stood together to the side. Harris wouldn't make eye contact with Claire or Nicole.

Claire saw Tony, Tessa, and Augustus sitting on a bench at the periphery of the crowd. The Corgis rested in the grass in front of them. The friends waved encouragingly from their seat.

Nicole reached for Claire's and Robby's hands and squeezed them so tightly Robby complained. "If you still want me to work for you after today, you're going to have to allow blood to flow into my hand."

"Sorry." Nicole had been around to look at the desserts she was competing against and reported to her friends that she had absolutely no chance. She'd seen some of the bakers walking around curiously looking at the other entries and when Nicole saw two of them she groaned. The husband and wife team who had won the past few years were entered again this year. "Why don't those two give someone else a chance? There's no way we can beat them. No way."

Robby mockingly praised her for being so optimistic.

Claire could feel Nicole shaking next to her.

"Our only chance at a medal is for third place and that's a long shot." Nicole sucked in a deep breath. "I'm never entering a contest again. Never. Don't ever try to make me."

Claire grinned, but said nothing.

The three celebrity judges, two men and a woman, took the stage to loud applause from the huge crowd gathered in front of the platform. The woman, perky and energetic, took the microphone and addressed the people telling them how difficult it was to choose, how wonderful all the desserts were, and on and on.

Nicole whispered, “Let’s get this over with.”

The gleaming wooden boxes containing huge medals were carried onto the stage and placed on a table with red, white, and blue skirting around it. One of the male judges opened a box and removed a shining, bronze medal with a two-inch red, white, and blue ribbon on it.

The band did a drum roll as the woman ceremoniously held the results card up, waited several seconds to draw out the suspense, and then announced the third place winner. It wasn’t Nicole’s chocolate shop.

Nicole’s shoulders drooped.

The people from the winning bakery stepped forward to accept the award and the male judge placed the ribboned medal over one person’s neck promising that the other baker would also receive a medal at the close of the day. The third-place winners shook hands with the organizers, posed for pictures, and then took their places back in the line of contestants.

The second place medal was announced and the procedure was repeated.

“Oh, well, maybe next year,” Nicole sighed.

Claire smiled and said softly, "A few minutes ago, you told us never to allow you to enter another contest."

Nicole squeezed Claire's hand. "My competitive juices have just kicked in."

When the first place, grand prize medal was awarded to the husband and wife team, the perky woman judge spoke loudly into the microphone before the crowd could disperse. "Hold on, everyone. For the first time in five years of the food festival, we have a tie for the first place grand prize. Our other grand prize winner is...." She let the words hang in the air for maximum drama. "From a North End shop ... *Chocolate Dreams*, Nicole Summers, Claire Rollins, and Robby Evans!"

Nicole yipped with surprise and as Robby and Claire stepped forward, a loud smash was heard. Claire glanced back to see Nicole passed out on the middle of the stage.

The crowd's loud applause was replaced with a collective gasp as people on the stage dashed to Nicole's side. Emergency medical personnel rushed up onstage to assist the fallen woman.

"She knows how to milk it, doesn't she?" Robby winked at Claire knowing nothing serious was wrong with his boss.

Claire's concern evaporated when she saw Nicole's eyes flutter open. "She is going to be mortified when she realizes she just fainted in front of hundreds of people."

"She is clever," Robby said. "Guess who will get top billing in the news reports of the winners?"

In a few minutes, Nicole was on her feet ... shaky feet, but upright at least. Robby and Claire each held an arm and maneuvered their friend to the awards' table to accept the gold medal. Claire noticed Ian standing at the front of the crowd and he waved and returned her smile.

Tears gathered in Nicole's eyes as the judge gently placed the award over her head and around her neck. The three chocolate shop bakers turned for pictures and to shake hands with the organizers. Claire was behind Nicole and Robby and she sucked in a breath as she reached for Ricky Harris's extended hand.

"Congratulations," he told her.

She thanked him and headed for the stairs behind her friends to exit the stage.

When Claire held Harris's hand, she felt something very much like what she'd sensed from Mel Watts when she met with him in his office. Harris knew more about Rose than he was telling them.

CLAIRE, Nicole, and Robby found their friends and the dogs and gathered around a table in the shade to cluck over Nicole's fainting spell.

"I feel so foolish." Nicole pressed her face into her palms.

After some good-natured kidding from Robby and Ian, she broke into giggles and had to admit that dropping unconscious to the stage floor would garner her some extra attention which she hoped would bring more notice to the chocolate shop.

"Great," Robby groaned and looked over at Claire. "Now the shop will get busier and we'll have to work harder, but I'll still get the same pay."

"Maybe we should mutiny," Claire laughed.

The group bought some appetizers of barbecue chicken wings, nachos, chicken strips, stir-fried rice, and stuffed mushrooms and they all feasted on the delights. Tony raised a cup of ginger ale and made a toast to the three successful contestants as the others lifted their soft drink and water containers in celebration. After an hour of chat, Tony, Tessa, and Augustus prepared to walk back to Tessa's car with the Corgis for the ride home.

Tessa leaned close to Claire. "How are things going on this case?"

Claire gave her the condensed version of what they'd learned so far.

"A number of suspects yet no clear feeling who the guilty party is." Tessa frowned.

"I get sensations from people, but they're all jumbled up and I can't sort out what it all means."

Tessa smiled. "You will. Let's talk soon. If you need some assistance, perhaps we can call on Maxwell again." Maxwell, an older man who was a friend of Tessa's, was a mysterious figure to Claire. The man had shown up outside a building where a death had occurred and reassured Claire that she was on the right track in her investigation.

"That might be very helpful," Claire said. "At the moment, I'm stumped."

When Tessa, Tony, Augustus, and the dogs went to their car, Ian got up from his seat and asked Claire to stroll around with him. Nicole told her to go ahead for a walk. "Robby and I will load the bakery supplies into the van. Then we'll go meet the organizers to pick up the additional medals for you and Robby. Meet in an hour or so?"

As Ian and Claire strolled the brick walkway along the harbor, a warm breeze floated over their skin. Ian raved about *Chocolate Dreams* winning the dessert contest.

"Co-won," Claire corrected with a smile.

"You three won the grand prize." Ian's eyes sparkled. "A co-win doesn't diminish the accomplishment. The shop will be buzzing with new customers now."

"Nicole better hire one of those applicants she's interviewed or we won't be able to handle the business." Claire let out a chuckle. "Customers will also come in just to see the woman who passed out when she found out she won."

"She'll never live that down."

The two bought ice cream cones from a vendor and continued their stroll.

"I know you have something to tell me," Claire said.

Ian looked sideways at the attractive blond next to him. "How do you know that?"

Claire gave the detective a sly look. "I can sense things." *If he only knew*, she thought.

"There is some security footage of Michael Burton and Rose Smith walking together in the financial district."

Claire's eyes widened. "How did you ever find

that film? Do you check every security camera in town whenever something happens?"

"It was pure luck." Ian licked his ice cream before it melted and ran down his wrist. "Officers were looking at tape for another case and noticed Burton."

"Where were they?"

"Not far from Burton's firm."

"Do they look like they're friendly with one another?"

"You mean like dating?" Ian asked. "No, they aren't holding hands, they're not close together. It looks more like two work colleagues walking together."

"Well, it discredits Michael's claim that he didn't know Rose well." Claire bit into her cone.

"Right. We're looking into the relationship." Ian glanced at Claire. "We're also trying to locate Rose. So far, no luck."

"She sent emails to her employees. Can you narrow down her whereabouts by looking at the computer's internet address?"

"We'd need a warrant to do that. We can't get a warrant based on the fact we think someone might be in danger."

"Do *you* think she's in danger?" Claire studied Ian's face.

"It's possible."

"It's why she's hiding somewhere." Claire nodded. "Rose thinks she's in danger because Ashley got killed. She thinks she was the intended target."

Ian kidded with Claire. "Is this something you're sensing?"

She looked directly into his eyes and told him the truth without him realizing it. "Yes."

They stopped by the water and sat on a bench to watch the boats in the harbor.

"Is Rose accessing her bank accounts?" Claire asked.

The corner of Ian's mouth turned up. "You know I can't tell you that."

"I'm going to guess that she is."

Ian remained silent as he worked on his ice cream.

"Can you tell me who's being considered as a suspect?"

"Nope."

"We talked to the husband today."

Ian shifted his eyes to Claire.

"I don't think he's being up front with us. I think he's withholding information."

"He might value his privacy."

"He might, but he seemed nervous talking about Rose." Claire shifted to face Ian. "Why would he be nervous?"

"Being nervous doesn't make the man guilty. People don't like to be put on the spot. He wasn't expecting to be asked questions about his wife. It made him uncomfortable."

Claire rested against the bench back. "Maybe he has more serious reasons to be nervous."

"Innocent until proven guilty," Ian reminded her.

"Trust no one," Claire countered.

"What about the benefit of the doubt?"

"You're a cop, you don't believe in the benefit of the doubt. And I'm suspicious, so neither do I."

"You don't mean that," Ian said.

Claire sighed. "I've recently discovered that the world can be a nasty place ... with terrible monsters in it."

Ian's kind eyes held Claire's. "It can also be a wonderful place, with even more wonderful people in it."

Claire's skin tingled as a flutter rushed through her veins and she had to hold herself back from resting her head gently against Ian's shoulder.

20

Claire took the elevator to the third floor and walked down the hall to the law office. She'd talked to Nicole at the chocolate shop about the need to find a friend of Rose Smith and decided to visit the receptionist they'd met in the law office next to Rose's office. After the shop closed for the day, Nicole was being interviewed by a news reporter about the win at the food festival so Claire was on her own.

The closer she got to the door of the law office, the harder her heart pounded and she didn't understand her apprehension. When she entered the reception area, she was glad to see the same woman sitting at her desk.

The receptionist, Abby Wilcox, glanced up and a wide smile spread over her face. "Oh, hi."

"Hi." Claire greeted her. "I was in a while ago asking about Rose."

"Sure. I remember. Where's your friend, the designer?"

Claire felt badly that they'd had to make up a story about Nicole being a designer. "She had a meeting this afternoon."

Abby nodded and then her face clouded. "I haven't seen Rose at all. I asked in the shop downstairs and they said she had to leave town for an emergency."

"I heard that, too."

"I don't know...." Abby's face screwed up in thought.

"What do you mean?"

"What emergency would Rose have to tend to?"

Claire cocked her in head in question.

"Rose's parents have passed away. She doesn't have any brothers or sisters. She told me she has no close relatives." Abby leaned forward. "Her husband lives here in the city. What kind of an emergency would Rose have to take care of?" Abby seemed to be expecting an answer from Claire.

"What about a friend?" Claire asked. "She might have gone to see a friend."

Abby bit her lower lip. "Rose doesn't really have any close friends."

"No one?"

"She has a friend who lives in Belgium. The woman was here a couple of months ago for a visit. Recently, Rose told me her friend was doing well so the emergency can't be about her." She gave a shake of the head. "I don't think Rose went to Belgium. She would have told me."

Claire was getting the distinct impression that Abby was closer to Rose than she'd let on during the first visit. "Have you heard from Rose? An email? A text?"

Abby's expression changed for a millisecond and then she said, "No, I haven't heard a word."

"I'm trying to get in touch with Rose. I came by to ask you if you knew of a friend I could contact. From what you said, I guess there isn't anyone in the city who would know anything?"

"I can't think of anyone." Abby's voice was soft.

Claire couldn't keep a sigh from slipping from her throat. She decided to come clean with the young woman. "Abby, I haven't exactly been upfront with you."

The receptionist stiffened.

"My friend, Nicole, isn't a designer. She runs a chocolate shop in the North End."

"Wait," Abby said. "She's the one who fainted at the food festival, right? I heard about it on the news. I thought she looked familiar."

"Nicole was on the news?"

"Yeah, last night." Abby gave Claire a look. "Why did you tell me she was a designer?"

"We need to talk to Rose. We can't find her. We're worried about her so we made up a story about wanting to meet with her and we thought it might seem legitimate if Nicole was a designer. I apologize."

Abby's face took on an expression of apprehension. "What was the real reason you wanted to see Rose?"

Claire took in a deep breath. "It's kind of a long story. Could we talk when you get out of work? Go to a coffee shop?"

Abby seemed be thinking it over. "You can talk to me now. Attorney Milliken is gone for the day. I'm the only one here." She gestured to the chair in the corner. "Pull up a seat."

Sitting across from the young woman, Claire began the tale. "I work with Nicole at the chocolate shop. I was walking to work early one morning and I saw a car pulled to the side of the lane. Something about its position and well, I don't know exactly, but I knew something was wrong. I moved closer so I could get a look inside. The window was open. The woman was dead. I found out later that her name was Ashley Smith."

"*You* found her?" Abby's eyes were wide.

"Nicole and I believe it was a case of mistaken identity." Claire went on to tell Abby how she ran into Rose one night at the crime scene. "Rose told me her legal name. I think Rose knows that she was the intended target."

Abby looked across the room and then turned back to Claire. "Are you with the police?"

"No." Claire shook her head. "I have a friend who is with the police force, but I'm a private citizen." She explained how she and Nicole had been involved in helping with two other crimes and why she had so many questions and concerns about Rose. "I found the body. I felt an obligation to find out why Ashley was killed. When I realized that Rose was in danger, I wanted to help her. I feel a duty."

"I'm worried, too." Abby blinked fast. "I'm worried about Rose."

"Have you talked to her?"

"No," Abby's voice was timid and Claire didn't

think she was being truthful, but also believed that the receptionist probably felt a duty to protect her friend.

Claire made eye contact with Abby. "Is there anything you can tell me that might help me figure out Ashley's death and Rose's sudden ... disappearance?"

Abby put her hands in her lap and looked down. "I'm not sure."

"What about her former partner, Mel Watts?"

Abby's head snapped up with an angry expression. "I did not like that guy. Rose did him a favor by taking him on. I didn't trust him. He could be really charming, but he is just a snake in the grass."

Claire's heart beat sped up. "Why do say this?"

"Why would this successful guy with holdings in real estate and in construction have an interest in fashion?" Abby's eyes flashed and she crossed her arms over her chest in a defensive posture. "Really? A guy in his position would act like an intern in Rose's business? I didn't buy it."

"But didn't he want to expand into other areas? Nicole and I met with him not long ago. We wanted to talk to him about Rose and if he knew how to contact her."

Abby said, "I bet he wasn't any help."

"He said he didn't know where Rose was," Claire said. "Watts told us he wanted to enter other fields of business and that's why he'd been working with Rose."

"I don't believe it." Abby's facial muscles were tense. "He's a CEO of a huge company. He'd hire some expert in the fashion industry if he wanted to expand."

Claire silently admonished herself for not taking that fact seriously and not being more suspicious about Watts's motivations for working with Rose. "Why do you think he wanted to work with Rose? What do you think was the real reason?"

Abby blew out a long breath. "I don't know. I told Rose my ideas, but she always thinks the best of people. At first, she thought I was being paranoid."

"Did she change her mind?"

"Over time, she grew not to trust his ideas or suggestions. She thought his talents didn't transfer well to her business. When she didn't want to go along with him on certain things, he got angry. She kept her eye on him and he didn't like that. Rose told me he was used to doing things his own way and didn't want to listen to her. She ended the partnership."

Claire sat up. "Rose ended it? Watts told me he was the one who ended it."

Abby's lips tightened into a line. "Watts is a liar."

"What about Rose's husband? Is their separation amicable?" Claire asked, her mind working over possibilities.

"Ricky is a selfish, self-centered child. He surrounds himself with good people who save his butt when he makes mistakes. Rose has helped him a lot with money. He is always overextending and Rose bails him out with loans from her business."

"Have you met Ricky?"

"Never. I have no interest in meeting him. That man takes advantage of Rose's kind and generous nature. Rose is a thousand times smarter than he is. He's so successful because of Rose."

"Has Rose been into the office this week?"

"No, she hasn't." Abby shook her head.

"Do you think it's possible Rose was the intended target of the killer who murdered Ashley Smith?"

Abby's hand passed over her eyes as she sighed heavily. "Maybe."

Claire had to ask the next question. "Did Rose have any involvement with Ashley's boyfriend, Michael Burton?"

Abby looked at Claire. “I don’t know anything about that.”

Claire leveled her eyes at Abby. “Do you know where Rose is?”

“No.” Abby didn’t hesitate in her response.

Claire was pretty sure she did know.

21

When Claire stepped out of the cab, she checked the time to see if the person she was looking for would be there. Entering the upscale South End bar, Claire glanced around and saw the man standing in front of three young women regaling them with some story about his escapades in the city.

Claire had employed Bob Cooney for a few hours about a month ago to break into an apartment in order to save someone's life. Cooney was thin, fit, and wiry, well-dressed in dark blue trousers and a pressed white shirt that was open at the collar. Several gold chains hung around his neck. In his mid-fifties, the man had dark brown eyes and jet black hair that didn't have a single strand of gray in it.

A private investigator by trade who didn't do much investigating these days, Cooney was known to be involved in many shady dealings, but always managed to come out clean. His involvement in things that weren't quite aboveboard had made him a very wealthy man.

Cooney spotted Claire from across the room and a shadow passed over his tanned face. Caught off guard, he paused, said something to his adoring fans, and walked to the far end of the bar which often seemed to double as his office.

"Wasn't expecting to see you." Cooney leaned on the bar and sipped from a small cocktail glass.

"You don't look too happy about it." Claire sidled up next to him.

"Got a problem? That why you're paying me a visit?" Cooney looked Claire up and down.

"Of sorts." She stood straight, with her shoulders back, and kept her voice even and firm to keep Cooney from trying to intimidate her.

The corners of the man's mouth turned down. "I don't think I can help you."

"You helped me last time I asked." Claire wanted to add, *and I paid you handsomely for it*, but she didn't think that would convince the man to talk to her so she refrained from saying anything about last time's payment.

"Here's the thing." Cooney placed his elbows on the glossy bar. "I don't care to assist the girlfriend of a Boston detective."

"Oh, that's what's bothering you." Claire eyed him. "First off, I'm not his girlfriend, we're friends, training buddies."

"Is that what you call it these days?" Cooney smirked. "*Training buddies*?"

"We compete in athletic events." Claire didn't know why she felt compelled to explain her association with Ian.

Cooney was about to say something sassy and off-color about "athletic events," but Claire raised her hand, palm forward. "Why don't we move away from this train of thought. The last time I employed you, I never said a word to the detective about what we did. I didn't mention your name."

Cooney swirled the liquid in his glass. "What do you want this time?"

"To talk. I have some questions I thought you might be able to clear up for me."

Cooney smiled showing his perfect white teeth. "Information isn't free, you know."

"I didn't expect it to be." Claire pushed her blond curls back from her face. "How much?"

"Depends on what you need clarification about."

Claire told him. "A murder. A case of mistaken identity. Does it sound familiar?"

"I don't know who killed the girl." Cooney's brow furrowed and he took a swallow of the alcohol in his glass.

"I'm not asking about that."

The man raised a questioning eyebrow wondering what she *was* going to ask about.

Claire said, "I wouldn't mind knowing who paid the killer to do the job."

"I wouldn't want to do your work for you," Cooney said. "It wouldn't be right. People need to develop a work ethic, learn to dig for information, put two and two together, use their reasoning skills." He shrugged a shoulder.

Claire wanted to bop him one. "Do you know Melvin Watts or Ricky Harris?"

Cooney gave Claire the eye. "I know who they are."

"Watts told Ricky's wife, Rose Smith, he wanted to learn the fashion business in order to expand into other areas of commerce. They formed a temporary partnership to work together so that Watts could get some experience." Claire watched Cooney's face. "The partnership ended sooner than planned."

"Not surprised." Cooney looked amused.

"Would you think that Watts had a legitimate interest in fashion boutiques?"

"Watts would have a legitimate interest in anything that made him money." Cooney drained his glass and raised a finger to the bartender indicating his desire for another drink.

"Wouldn't he hire someone with strong experience in the field of interest instead of partnering with Rose?"

"You'd think so, wouldn't you?" Cooney's drink arrived and he picked it up and sipped. The bartender looked at Claire, but she shook her head.

"I don't think he'd take time out of his other pursuits to work with Rose," Claire said.

"I think you'd be right." Cooney smiled at two chesty blondes at the other end of the bar.

Claire moved to position herself in his line of vision. If she was going to have to pay the man for the conversation, she wanted his undivided attention. "Then why would he do it?"

"It's my turn to ask some questions." Cooney adjusted his collar and gold necklaces.

"Okay." Claire waited.

"Why would a guy like Watts form a temporary partnership?" Cooney asked.

"I assume for some sort of financial gain," Claire responded.

"Why the temporary part?" Cooney pressed.

"Because he would get what he wanted in a certain period of time and then he'd move on," Claire answered.

"Bingo. You get a gold star." Cooney moved slightly to the side so he could ogle the women at the bar.

"I had that figured out already," Claire told the man.

"Okay, then. What's Watts's specialty? He runs a real estate investment company, but what is his experience in?"

"I don't know." Claire's shoulder went up in a shrug.

Watts gestured to her phone. "Look it up."

Claire scowled and tapped at her phone to do a search on Watts. "Finance. He started at a financial company, did fraud investigations, things like that. Then he moved to another company, worked with hedge funds. He left to join a real estate and construction firm. He stayed there for two years and then he established his own company." She looked up. "So? I knew most of that."

Cooney rolled his eyes. "You're supposed to be smart, Rollins. You've got a law degree. Think."

Claire narrowed her eyes. "How do you know I have a law degree?"

"I know a lot of things. Use your reasoning skills, put two and two together. I'll wait."

Annoyance bubbled up in Claire's chest, but if she didn't play the game, she wasn't going to get anywhere. She looked down at the phone and re-read the information on Watts. Something pinged in her head. "Finance. Fraud. Watts was doing something with Rose's finances?"

Cooney cocked his head. "I'll give you a B+ for that."

Claire tried to make sense of what she read and knew. Things swirled around in her mind, but she couldn't grasp the answer. "Do you know what Watts was up to?"

"No. But I'd bet he had his hands in Rose's cookie jar and if I were you, I'd follow that path and see where it leads." Cooney picked up his drink. "Now, I must return to what I was doing." Tapping his finger on the bar, he stared at Claire and she sighed.

"How much?" she asked.

When Cooney told her his fee, her face hardened. "That's ridiculous," she fumed.

The man said, "And here is a little lesson for the day ... agree on the fee before the work begins."

Claire made a face. "What if I can't afford it?"

"Here's the second lesson of the day ... know who you're dealing with before dealing with them." Cooney smiled. "I did my research after our last business transaction. I *know* you can afford it."

Claire did not like that Cooney looked into her finances and had some idea that she had plenty of money. She would like to know how he found out and who helped him, but she understood there was no point in asking.

In anticipation of Cooney's high fees, Claire had been to the bank before arriving at the bar. With another sigh, she dug into her bag, counted the money so no one could see what she was doing, and handed it to the man. "Thanks for the discussion."

"Any time." Cooney started to saunter away to join the women standing at the end of the bar, but turned back for a moment with a serious expression. "Listen, Rollins, there are some people in this world who don't think like you do. They'd do anything to get what they want. Anything. In order to figure stuff like this out, you need to think like someone with a twisted, devious mind. Someone who only cares about one or two things ... money ... or power ... or both."

With that, Cooney gave Claire a nod and walked away.

22

Claire and Nicole sat under the shade tree on the patio eating macaroni and cheese with tomatoes and broccoli, green salad, and garlic bread while the Corgis sniffed along the fence and watched a squirrel high on the branches. Claire told Nicole about her visits to Abby Wilcox and Bob Cooney.

"It was pretty clear that Abby is a friend of Rose and I'm pretty sure she knows where Rose is."

"Abby is protecting her." Nicole reached for the jug of iced tea and poured some into her glass. "How was our buddy, Mr. Cooney?" The man's behavior the last time the two friends met with him and his reputation for misdeeds had left Nicole with a bad taste and she preferred never to interact with him again.

"The usual." Claire rolled her eyes. "He did say some things that made a lot of sense though. He told me I needed to think like someone with a devious and twisted mind."

Nicole stopped chewing and held her fork in the air. "Even though that sounds really awful, Cooney is right. We need to start thinking like the evil-doers."

"So what do we do? Pretend we don't care about anything? Pretend we have no values or morals?"

Nicole said, "I guess so." Thinking about it, she asked, "How do we start?"

Claire looked up at the inky blue of the darkening sky. "Let's start with Mel Watts. It doesn't make any sense that he would want to work closely with Rose. Like we've said, he'd hire someone to develop that additional business. So what was he doing?"

"Obviously, it must have to do with money."

"Right. Was he stealing from Rose?" Claire asked.

"It seems that he must have been."

"Why pick Rose to get involved with?"

Nicole thought about it. "Maybe he thought he could manipulate her easily? Hide things from her without her finding out?"

Claire asked, "Wouldn't that mean Watts had to know Rose fairly well in order to think she was an easy mark? He had to know her well to even propose the idea of temporarily working together, wouldn't he? She probably agreed to it as a favor to him."

Nicole narrowed her eyes. "Or as a favor to someone else."

"Rose's husband? Watts told us he didn't know Ricky Harris well."

"We need to think like a deviant," Nicole reminded Claire. "Is Watts lying about how well he knew Ricky? To throw us off?"

Claire went inside to get her laptop and did a search on the two men. Her face took on a hard look. "Why didn't we research those two earlier? Look at this." She turned the screen for Nicole to see, thinking how Cooney told her to know who she was dealing with before she had to deal with them. "Look at all the pictures of these guys together. There's even one with Watts at Rose and Ricky's wedding." Rubbing her temples, she asked, "Why didn't I pick up on this?"

"Well, you did, sort of." Nicole scrolled through the information on the laptop. "You were sure that Watts and Ricky Harris were holding back information from us."

"Are those two working together? Did they steal money from Rose's business?" Claire groaned. "I want to talk to Abby Wilcox again. Maybe Rose had money concerns and talked to Abby about it."

Lady rubbed her nose against Claire's bare leg and made her jump. She chuckled and reached down to pat the sweet dog. "You want to go for a walk? We missed our walks today, didn't we?"

"That's a good idea. It's a nice evening. Let's go walk." Nicole stood up to clear the table. "We need a break from murder and misfortune."

After loading the dishwasher and washing pans in the sink, the young women got the leashes from the closet and set off with the dogs down the brick sidewalks.

"We're not allowed to talk about anything related to what's been going on," Nicole announced.

Claire agreed. "Did you decide on any of the people you interviewed to work in the shop?"

"Not yet. With the food festival and this case, I feel like I've been running in circles. We've had an increase in customers since we won at the festival so I'd better get on the ball and hire some new people or we aren't going to be able to keep up with things." Nicole stopped to let Bear sniff at the curb. "The gold medals for you and Robby are in and ready to be picked up. I got an email saying the receptionist in Ricky Harris's office has them." Because of the first place tie, the organizers hadn't ordered enough medals for the winners.

"We can go by later in the week," Claire suggested.

They turned onto the street where Ashley's and Rose's townhouse building was located. Claire looked up at the penthouse apartment. "Wouldn't it be a stroke of good luck if Rose had returned to her place and we saw her in the window?"

All the windows of the apartment were dark.

"No such luck," Nicole said.

Claire stopped short and her friend eyed her. Nicole was about to ask why she'd stopped walking, when Claire turned around abruptly. Someone was heading down the sidewalk towards them.

When the man got close, his eyes widened. "Oh, hi." It was Michael Burton.

"We thought you'd left town," Nicole said. "You haven't moved away yet?"

"I'm still here."

"Did you change your mind about leaving?" Claire asked.

"No." Michael took a look at the Corgis. "I need to wait a little while longer to leave."

"Why?" Nicole asked, even though she felt it was rude and prying.

Michael blew out a breath. "The police asked me to stick around ... to answer any questions that might come up."

Claire suspected that the police didn't want a possible suspect leaving town. Little electric pulses bounced over her skin and made her uneasy. "Can we talk? Can you go with us to the coffee shop?"

Michael glanced at his building and shuffled from foot to foot. "I don't have much to say."

"We won't keep you long," Claire said. "It might be helpful to talk." The man was about to decline, when she added, "I have some things to tell you." Claire wanted to observe the man's reaction to what she planned to say.

Michael looked at Claire. "I guess I could. You want to come up? I can make some coffee."

When they entered the man's apartment, they saw the place was nearly bare of furniture. Only a small table sat by the windows and there was one leather chair in front of the fireplace.

"I've sold almost everything." Michael gestured to the table and four chairs. "Have a seat. I'll get the coffee."

The dogs, on edge, sniffed around the room.

Once they were settled at the table, Claire wasn't sure where to start. "We've talked to several people in connection with Ashley's death and Rose's disappearance."

Michael said, "The police told me it was a case of the killer shooting the wrong person."

Nicole nodded. "Rose was the target. That's why she took off."

Claire shared what they'd learned from Abby Wilcox, Mel Watts, Ricky Harris, and the employees at Rose's boutique. "We know that you and Ashley were probably going to split up. We also heard through the grapevine that you and Rose were acquainted with one another."

Michael was about to protest, but then he shrugged a shoulder. "We weren't involved with one another. It wasn't like that."

"What *was* it like?" Claire asked gently. "We're trying to help figure out what's going on, to figure out who's after Rose."

Michael looked down at his mug. "Rose knew where I worked, what I did for work. She asked me to help with her business finances. She thought something was wrong."

Claire and Nicole exchanged a look.

"She was working with Mel Watts," Claire said. "We heard it was a temporary partnership."

Michael gave a nod.

"Did you help Rose?"

"I did."

"Did you find anything amiss?" Nicole questioned.

Michael took a gulp of his coffee and set the mug down hard. "I don't know what to do. Rose told me my investigation into the finances had to be done confidentially. I couldn't reveal what I found out to anyone. She even told me not to tell the police anything." He let out a short burst of mirthless laughter. "I thought that was ridiculous. Why would the police ever ask me anything?" Sadness dragged at his face. "I promised Rose I would keep whatever I discovered in confidence. Now I don't think I can."

Claire's heart started to race. "You found irregularities in her finances?"

Michael gave the slightest of nods. "Her business was bleeding cash. It happened suddenly, well, not so suddenly. Things started slowly and built over a few months. It took time to find it. Someone was stealing from Rose. At first, I thought it was the bookkeeper, but then I wasn't so sure. Rose wouldn't let me interview anyone. I couldn't call attention to anything. Rose seemed real nervous about it. She wanted me to take a look and not to let on to anyone that we suspected wrongdoing."

"Do you know who was responsible?" Nicole asked.

"Not really. I wasn't given the necessary access to determine who was doing it. Then Ashley got killed, and Rose took off."

"Did Rose tell you who she thought was stealing from her?" Claire asked.

"She didn't mention anyone's name. I told her she needed to hire an accountant who specializes in this kind of thing to figure out what was going on. It's not my specialty." Michael looked from Claire to Nicole. "I've been torn about keeping this quiet. Should I tell the police what I found?"

"Yes," Claire nodded. "You should talk to them."

"If I tell them, will it put Rose in jeopardy?"

Claire said, "I think she's already in jeopardy. Your information might assist the police in helping her."

As Claire stood up to go, her hand brushed against Michael's arm causing a flash of anxiety to race through her body.

23

Claire entered Ricky Harris's office on the sixth floor of a glass and brick building in the financial district. It wasn't as large or fancy as Mel Watts's office, but it was decorated in cool blues and grays and had framed photographs on the walls of Ricky at food events and charity events posing with important and well-known celebrities and politicians.

Claire explained that she was there to pick up the medals they'd won at the festival a few days ago.

"Oh, right." The receptionist was a cute, young, outgoing, woman in her early twenties. "I don't have them here, they're in Ricky's office." She smiled and pointed down the hall. "Just go down and knock. He's in there. He'll want to take a picture with you, I bet."

Claire's heart dropped. The last thing she wanted was to see Ricky Harris and she thought he probably felt the same way. "Oh, well, I don't...."

"Go ahead." The receptionist waved her hand. "Don't be shy. You aren't bothering him. Ricky loves to talk to bakers and chefs."

Unable to think of a way to get out of it, Claire plastered a smile on her face and shuffled away down the hall. She passed two open doors and peeked in as she walked by. The next door had a black metal nameplate on it, *Ricky Harris.*

Claire took a deep breath and raised her hand to knock, but hesitated when she heard his voice behind the door speaking to someone on the phone.

Ricky said with exasperation, "I don't know where Rose is. If I did, I'd have the money. Why can't you be patient? You know I'm good for it. Rose will lend it to me. She always does." The man went quiet, obviously listening to the person on the other end of the call.

"This is my brand," Ricky said in reply. "You know what it's worth. As soon as I can borrow from Rose, I'll be all set. She always helps me out when I'm in a pinch. I know, I know. There have been a lot of expenses that have come up all at the same time. Don't worry about it. Rose will help me out."

Claire heard Ricky hit the top of his desk in annoyance with what the person on the phone had said and she decided to slink away.

When she reached the reception area, the young woman looked up with a bright smile. "That was quick. Did you get the medals?"

"No." Claire edged towards the door. "Ricky was on the phone. I'll come back another time. I work nearby."

The receptionist was about to protest, but Claire opened the door and exited. Hurrying out of the elevator to the sidewalk, her mind was twirling trying to make sense of what she'd heard.

If Ricky and Mel were stealing from Rose, why was Ricky low on cash? Was Mel actually the one who was stealing and doing it on his own? Was Ricky innocent of any wrongdoing or was he putting on a show of having no money?

The late afternoon breeze blew off the ocean causing goosebumps to form over Claire's arms. Deep in thought, she turned the corner and almost plowed into an oncoming pedestrian.

The woman stepped quickly to the side to avoid a crash and when she saw who was in front of her, she said, "Claire."

Claire blinked a few times trying to remember

the familiar young woman. "Oh, Meg." It was Ashley Smith's friend who had come to Tony's market to find Claire and share her concerns about Michael Burton.

"Listen, I'm glad I ran into you." Meg's face was sad and drawn. "I was going to come talk to you again. Do you have a few minutes? Could we sit in the park for a little while?"

Claire wanted to hurry to Nicole's apartment to tell her what she'd heard Ricky Harris saying on the phone, but Meg seemed so forlorn, she couldn't deny the woman a few minutes. "Sure," she said reluctantly. "Let's go find a bench."

"I'm feeling awful." Meg put her tote bag on the bench beside her, removed a tissue, and dabbed at her eyes. "No one's been arrested in Ashley's murder. How long does it take? When will they find the person who did this?"

Claire explained that the police were still investigating and wouldn't give up. She tried to comfort Meg by telling her how so many leads had to be followed, that the case wasn't closed, that little things would turn up and lead to the killer. Claire hoped so anyway.

"I know, I know." Meg crumpled the tissue in her

fist. "It's just that it seems so hopeless, like trying to find a needle in haystack."

Claire smiled. "But that's what the police do. They find that needle and they solve the crime."

Meg looked wistfully at Claire. "But some crimes are never solved. That's my fear about Ashley. She was such a great person. They have to find her killer ... they just have to."

Claire gently touched the woman's arm. "Hold on to hope. That's all we can do."

Meg clutched her hands tightly in her lap and looked out over the park.

"Did you go to the police and tell them your concerns about Ashley's boyfriend, Michael?" Claire asked. Sitting next to Meg caused her body to pulse with anxiety as if her nerves were firing wildly.

Meg gave a nod. "I did. I told them my worries."

"Good. It's good you talked to them. You've done what you could to help."

"I don't think I did enough."

Claire took a close look at Meg.

"I ... I know something else that I haven't shared," Meg said.

Claire's throat tightened. "You do?"

A tear escaped from Meg's eye and traced down

her cheek. "Ashley grew up in a very strict, religious household. Her father was a preacher. Her parents are dead, but they still held influence over Ashley and how she felt about herself."

Claire could barely contain herself and wished Meg would blurt out what she had to say. Meg didn't continue so Claire asked, "How do you mean?"

Meg cleared her throat. "Ashley confided in me. She told me not to tell a soul. Ashley was pregnant."

Claire's blue eyes widened. "It was Michael's?"

"Yes. Ashley was devastated at his reaction."

"What happened?" Claire's head was spinning.

"Michael made it plain that he did not want a child. They discussed it. Michael said that Ashley would have to take care of the baby on her own. He would help financially, but he still wanted an open relationship."

"He'd marry Ashley?"

"They hadn't got that far yet. It was up in the air. Ashley thought that Michael would marry her, but because he wanted to be free to go out with other women, she would have to handle child duties." Meg sighed and shook her head. "Ashley thought that once the baby was born, then Michael would change and they'd become a family. I knew that wasn't going to happen."

Claire asked, "When you talked to the police, did you tell them that Ashley was pregnant?"

Meg blinked back tears. "No. I know it's stupid, but Ashley didn't want anyone to know so I didn't think I should say anything about it."

Claire said, "I assume an autopsy was done on Ashley so the police must know about the pregnancy."

Meg wrapped her arms around herself. "I don't think they do."

Claire gave Meg a questioning look.

"Ashley lost the baby two weeks before she died."

"Did Michael know she'd lost the baby?" Claire asked.

"No. She hadn't told him yet."

"Does Michael know that Ashley told you about the pregnancy?"

"Absolutely not. Ashley didn't tell him that I knew. She told him no one knew."

Claire's stomach clenched. "Go to the police. Tell them what you know. I think it's important. Will you do that?"

"Yes," Meg almost whispered. "I will."

~

CLAIRE HEADED down Newbury Street and turned at the corner to the building that housed Rose's boutique and the law office where Abby Wilcox worked. Even though Abby had told Claire in their first meeting that she didn't know anything about Michael Burton, Claire felt that Abby opened up more the last time they talked and she might be willing to reveal some more information.

Not wanting to barge into the law office again, Claire waited on the sidewalk across from the building knowing that in thirty minutes they would close for the day. Leaning on the trunk of a tree, she watched the people walking by and kept an eye on the front door in case Abby left early.

When she glanced up to Rose's office window, Claire had the impression that the shadow of someone walked past. She stared at the glass for a few minutes and decided it was only the sunlight that had caused the impression.

Claire had been watching the window and almost missed Abby when she stepped out from the door and started away. Hurrying across the street to catch up with the young woman, Claire called her name. Abby turned around with an annoyed look. When she saw Claire, she frowned and didn't say a word.

"Can I walk with you?" Claire smiled. "I wanted to talk a little."

Abby's face was hard. "I can't now. I have to be somewhere."

"Is something wrong?"

"Nothing. I need to go. I can't talk." Abby whirled and stormed away.

"Abby?" Claire took a few steps forward.

The young woman glared at Claire. "I said I can't."

Claire stood staring after her, baffled by the behavior when a thought popped into her head. *Rose must have told Abby not to talk to me.*

Feeling dejected and down, Claire headed for home. She wanted to stop at Tony's to talk things over and she wanted to hear Nicole's take on the news that Ashley had been pregnant.

Suspects and motivations swirled around in Claire's mind. One minute, she was sure it was a particular person and then, the next minute, she settled on someone else. Her head started to pound and she rubbed at the back of her neck. Walking through the Public Garden in the evening light, a heavy sense of fatigue washed over her.

She crossed the street and headed up Beacon Hill, and when she was a block from Ashley,

Michael, and Rose's building, a sense of panic raced through her veins. *What's wrong with me?*

Claire had to drag her feet up the sidewalk and the closer she got to the townhouse, the more each step made her feel like she was going to her doom. She stopped and pulled out her phone, but didn't know what she would tell whoever she ended up calling so she stuffed it back in her bag.

The streetlight came on and Claire stood under its pale, yellow light, the sky still a dark indigo blue. She thought how she'd walked past Ashley's building a million times and never had this sensation.

Taking slow, deliberate steps, Claire moved to stand across the street from the house that was making her feel sick and weak. Looking at the windows of Michael's apartment, an image flashed in her brain that sent her stumbling backwards. Vertigo made her clutch a lamp post as panic flew in her chest.

Her vision dimming, she rummaged for her phone, pulled it out, and about to punch in Ian's number, the phone fumbled in her trembling hands. It hit the sidewalk and skittered over the bricks, fell off the curb, and dropped between the slats of the sewer grate.

Claire's heart sank as she raised her eyes to the third floor windows.

I have to go in there.

24

Maybe the door will be locked and I won't be able to get in, Claire thought as she climbed the few steps to the front of the building. Like the last time she was there, the door hadn't clicked all the way shut and she was able to walk into the lobby.

She hurried to the first floor apartment and knocked on the door hoping to ask the occupant to call '911.' No one answered so she rushed up the stairs and pounded on the second floor apartment door. When no one replied to her knock, Claire's eyes filled with tears.

Shaking like a leaf and feeling faint, she grasped the banister and pulled herself up to the third floor where she moved her feet slowly and softly over the landing to Michael Burton's door.

The sound of anger ricocheted off the walls inside the apartment ... a man's and a woman's voices. Claire put her ear close to the door. The woman's words were muffled, but the tone was accusatory and frightened.

"I did it for you." Michael Burton's voice was loud and had an edge of hysteria to it.

"Michael," the woman whimpered. "*You* had Ashley killed? Because of me? I don't understand what you've done."

Michael growled, "I love you and you love me."

"No, no." The woman sobbed. "No."

Claire's throat tightened and her heart beat pounded in her ears. She knew that things were about to go very wrong.

The woman spoke again, but her words were choked with tears so Claire couldn't make out what she'd said.

Heavy footsteps moved around the apartment.

"Michael!" the woman shrieked. "No!"

"You aren't going to tell the police," Michael's voice boomed. "I won't let you ruin everything I've worked so hard for."

"Don't. Don't do this...." The woman's tone was one of desperation.

Sucking in a long breath, Claire raised her fist and pounded on the door.

Silence in the apartment.

"Who's there?" Michael demanded.

"Open this door." Claire deepened her voice to sound authoritative and pounded again. Nothing happened. "Michael Burton, open this door!"

The door flew open. Michael stood before her, looking crazed and disheveled. Rose Smith stood meekly to the side, tears glistening on her cheeks. Confusion washed over the man's face as he struggled to decide if Claire could possibly be a member of law enforcement.

Claire said the first thing that came into her head. "Michael Burton, the police have a warrant for your arrest."

Rose hurried to Claire's side, her face pale, her shoulders hunched.

"Step back," Claire roared at the man. She hoped her command would cause Michael to move further into the apartment so that she and Rose could make their escape down the stairs.

Michael stood his ground, glaring at Claire, his arm held slightly behind his back.

"He has a gun," Rose whispered to Claire.

Michael made a decision. He brought his arm

around and pointed the gun at Claire and Rose. "Where's your badge, Claire?"

Claire stepped in front of Rose as she told Michael, "Rose and I are going to leave and you're going to stay in your apartment."

"No." Michael's face hardened. "You're not. Shut the door."

When Claire didn't move, Michael pointed at the ceiling and pulled the trigger. With a blast, a bullet drove through the plaster into the upper floor.

Michael began to pant. "Shut the door or the next bullet will go through Rose's heart."

Claire kicked the door shut with her foot and stayed positioned in front of Rose.

"What are you doing, Michael?" Claire asked him. "You're only making it worse for yourself."

His breathing was fast and shallow and the man looked like a wild animal ready to pounce.

"I know what you've done." Claire tried to make her voice sound calm. "The police know what you've done," she fibbed. "They'll be here soon with an arrest warrant."

"How do you know that?" Spit flew out of the man's mouth. "Why did *you* come here?"

Claire's mind raced. How was she going to get out of this? How would she get Rose out of this? An idea took form. She would try to frighten Michael by telling him the truth.

"You want to know why I came here?" She swallowed hard. "I came because I knew something was wrong in this apartment. I came because I know what you did. I can *feel* it, Michael. It's all floating on the air."

Claire took a step forward. "I have an unusual skill. I can *sense* things, my instinct is strong." Knowing this was either going to work or it was going to be the end of her, Claire kept talking. "I know that Ashley was pregnant. I know you didn't want her or the baby. I know that you're attracted to Rose. I know that you wanted an open relationship so you could try to be with Rose."

She took another step forward. "I'm a psychic, Michael. Yes. I work with the police. Your secrets are out." Claire's voice grew louder. "I know that you manipulated Ashley so that she would put you in her will because of the baby. I know there was life insurance ... and you wanted it."

Michael's face paled. He looked at Claire like she was a demon.

"I know you manipulated Rose so that she would trust you," Claire went on winging her accusations and hoping her ideas were correct. "You made the whole terrible murder seem like mistaken identity. You frightened Rose into thinking that someone was stealing from her, you hired someone to kill Ashley to get rid of her and the baby, and by planting the seed that Ashley was killed by mistaken identity, you made Rose believe *she* was the intended victim. I'll even guess that you made Rose believe her husband and Melvin Watts were working together to steal her money and were planning to kill her."

Michael started to shake. As he ran his hand through his hair, his wild eyes darted around the room, but he still held the gun and pointed it at Claire.

"Put the gun down, Michael. Don't make it worse for yourself. The police will be here any minute." Claire wished the last sentence was true. "Just place it on the floor and step back."

The expression on the man's face made it seem that he didn't understand a word Claire was saying.

"I'm going to ask Rose to leave now. I'll stay with you." Claire watched the man and then she touched Rose gently on the arm to move her towards the door. She turned her head a little and whispered, "Call the police."

While Rose took hold of the door handle and turned it, Claire used a soothing voice, "Rose is going to leave. It's going to be okay. I'll stay with you until the police come. That way, they won't hurt you, Michael. I'll walk out with you when they come."

Rose stepped out into the hallway and Claire spoke again to distract the man from focusing on the woman's exit. "Michael, why don't we both sit down. I'm going to sit down on the floor. Everything will be okay."

Claire slipped down to seated position on the wood floor. "Sit with me, Michael."

Beads of sweat ran down the sides of Michael's face. His cheeks had changed from pale to bright red. He muttered words that Claire couldn't understand.

Claire's hands were freezing, her head buzzed, her ears rang. Everything seemed to slow. Endless minutes ticked by. She just wanted it to be over. *Don't shoot me, don't shoot me.*

Michael was still standing, his arm hung down loosely at his side and the hand holding the gun twitched as if it was being shocked. Taking a small step, his legs almost went out from under him. His eyes flashed around the near-empty room at the one chair and the one remaining table.

Michael wobbled and headed for the bedroom, stumbling out of the living room. Claire watched him go and then pushed herself up off the floor. She listened.

She backed up inching to the door.

Time seemed frozen as she moved so slowly, sliding her feet backwards into the hall, keeping her eyes glued towards the bedroom. She heard footsteps on the staircase and in ten seconds, two Boston police officers were at her side. Relief flooded through her body making her feel weak.

"He's in the bedroom," Claire told them quietly. "He has a gun."

Just as the officers advanced into the apartment with their weapons drawn, a horrible blast sounded in the bedroom. The terrible noise rocked the walls and sent a wave of disbelief and dread smashing into Claire.

She covered her mouth and whirled towards the staircase just as someone rushed up the stairs, took hold of the shaken young woman, and with his strong arms wrapped tight around her, pulled her close.

Ian.

Claire rested her cheek against his chest, gripped him like a drowning woman, and began to weep.

25

Ian manned the grill in the small backyard of Claire's townhouse while Tessa, Tony, and Augustus sat at the table sipping their drinks under the twinkling lights on the big tree's branches. The Corgis sat one on each side of Tony's chair and he had both arms hanging down to pet the dogs' heads.

Bear and Lady had their noses pointed up inhaling the delicious smell of the kebobs, skewers of vegetables, and hamburgers and hot dogs cooking over the charcoal. The early evening air was warm and pleasant and the first distant stars sparkled against the navy blue sky.

Robby and Nicole worked in the kitchen recreating the co-winning dessert from the food festival and Claire carried out a plate of appetizers. Before setting it on the table, she offered some to Ian who selected a stuffed mushroom and popped it into his mouth. When his eyes met Claire's, little sparks jumped between them.

Nicole and Robby emerged from the house to join the others on the patio.

"The desserts are in the fridge," Nicole announced. "They'll be ready when we finish dinner."

"They came out great, too." Robby grinned and shoved the remaining part of the custard he'd stolen from the platter into his mouth.

They took seats at the table with their friends and joined in the discussion about the case.

As his world crumbled around him, Michael Burton took his own life. He had indeed hired a hit man to kill his girlfriend, Ashley Smith, with the assumption being that the man couldn't handle the responsibilities of a committed relationship or of being a father. He had become fixated on and obsessed with Rose Smith and was determined to have her as his love.

Ashley, Michael, and Rose had met in their building and had gathered in each other's apartments for drinks many times. When Rose became concerned about her business's outflow of money and knowing both Ashley and Michael were in the financial industry, she consulted them about what might be going on.

Even though Michael wasn't fully experienced in such things, he offered to investigate the boutique's bookkeeping.

Michael told Rose that her finances looked suspicious and that someone was probably stealing from her suggesting the culprit could be Mel Watts. He even planted the idea that Rose's ex-husband was in on it.

As it turned out, Mel *was* siphoning off money from Rose's business and directing it to his own accounts. Although her husband had spoken to Rose suggesting she allow Mel to work with her for a period of time, Ricky was not involved in the financial deception and had himself wondered if Mel was up to something.

When Ashley was killed, Michael told Rose that he feared *she* was the intended victim and convinced her that Mel and Ricky were most likely behind it. Rose was terrified that Michael was right ... she didn't trust Mel and Ricky always had money crises and could easily be led astray under certain circumstances. She thought Ricky might be involved in stealing from her, but she'd recently heard terrible things about Mel Watts and believed he was acting alone to get rid of her.

She panicked and took off.

Rose returned from hiding when Michael emailed her and said he'd found evidence that Mel Watts was the person who wanted her dead. In actuality, he had no such evidence.

Michael wanted to reveal his love for Rose and had planned that she would accompany him out of the country. When Rose heard what Michael had done, she nearly collapsed in horror.

She told him he needed help and that she had to tell the police that he was responsible for Ashley's murder. That's when Claire showed up at the door.

When Ashley learned she was pregnant, she changed her will and took out a life insurance policy naming Michael as the beneficiary hoping her devotion and trust would encourage him to accept the baby and marry her.

Bradford Bilson from the financial firm had contacted Claire in regards to his murdered employee because he'd been informed that Ashley and Michael seemed to be having trouble with their relationship and it had been interfering with their work. An associate had also reported to Bilson that

Michael had been acting erratically the day before Ashley was killed.

After hours of tireless investigation, the police considered Michael Burton a serious suspect, but they didn't have enough evidence against the man to formally charge him.

The investigators also had a person of interest on their radar, the hit man hired by Michael Burton to kill his girlfriend, and would soon be bringing him in for questioning. A few minor details were left to be ironed out, but the hope was that the man would be charged with murder.

"Melvin Watts will now spend some time behind bars for funneling money from Rose's business accounts to his own off-shore accounts," Augustus said. "The man has been suspected for years of such misdeeds, and for far worse things than embezzlement, but he has always managed to keep the allegations from sticking to him." The older man's eyes sparkled. "This time, Mr. Watts was unable to outrun his villainy."

"It baffles me how people like Mel Watts and Michael Burton exist," Tony grumped. "How can people do such evil things to each other?"

"They are troubled men," Tessa said sadly, "who

unfortunately wreaked havoc and misfortune on many lives."

Nicole smiled at Claire and, referring to the phone that dropped into the sewer the night her friend went to Michael Burton's apartment, she said, "From now on, Claire needs to keep two phones with her at all times."

Claire shook her head making her long curls bounce around her face. "I replaced the phone. I didn't think about getting two of them."

"You did a remarkable job, Blondie." Tony gave her a warm smile. "You saved Rose ... and yourself. Thank heavens. But you shouldn't have gone into that apartment alone."

Claire exchanged a look with Tessa. She couldn't tell the man about her intuition and why she'd been so compelled to go up to Michael's place that night so all she said was, "You're right. I shouldn't have."

"You sure convinced Burton that you were a psychic." Robby winked at the woman he called Clairvoyant Claire.

Claire glared at him, not wanting that piece of information to get any attention.

Ian brought a dish of shish-kebobs to the table and gave Claire a look. "You also convinced Rose you were a psychic."

Giving a nervous chuckle, Claire made up a tale to cover for what she'd told Michael Burton. "I was desperate and grasping at straws. I'd read an article that morning about a psychic and it popped into my mind when I was talking to Michael. I couldn't think of anything else that might throw him off so I told him I had paranormal powers."

"Well, nicely done." Ian held the pretty blonde's eyes which made her heart skip a beat.

Everyone squished around the table and dug into the food enjoying the delicious meal and conversation. The Corgis received plates of meat and veggies and they gobbled up the dinner with gusto.

When the table was cleared and the dishwasher loaded, Nicole removed the tray of chocolate swirl custards and placed the Florentine cookies into the tops. Claire set the table with small white dessert plates and silver forks and spoons.

"The winning desserts," Tony's voice boomed announcing the arrival of the sweet part of the meal.

When Tessa scooped a spoonful of the custard into her mouth, she closed her eyes and moaned. "No wonder you won first prize."

"The Florentine cookie is just like my grandmother made for me when I was a little boy," Augustus told the group. He nodded. "Thank you to the bakers for bringing back lovely thoughts of my childhood."

Robby ate two of the desserts and was going for a third when Nicole bopped him. "Wait and see if someone else would like a second one," she scolded.

"Let the young man have it." Tony patted the little bit of a stomach that showed under his shirt. "I must keep my trim figure."

"I don't need to be encouraged a second time." Robby helped himself to his third dessert.

When everyone was satisfied and full, Ian asked to see the medal awarded at the festival and Claire went inside to retrieve it. "I finally went to see Ricky Harris to pick them up." The huge gold medal was passed from person to person and each one oohed and aahed over it.

"This is only the beginning," Tony said. "I see more accolades in the future."

"A writer for a Boston magazine got in touch with me. He wants to interview me and Claire and Robby." Nicole beamed. "More advertising for the chocolate shop."

"Is the writer interviewing the co-first-place winners, too?" Ian asked.

"No. He said because the other winners had received the first place award for the past few years, he wanted to focus on the up and comers." Nicole seemed to deflate a little. "I ran into the owners of the other bakery that took the other first place award. I saw them in the Back Bay and went over to talk. They got up abruptly and wouldn't speak to me other than saying hello. They actually glared at me. They gave me the creeps."

"I guess they don't like sharing the first place position," Augustus noted. "They must feel you have knocked them from their pedestal."

"It was weird." Nicole sipped from her tea cup. "I hope I never run into them again."

"They must be very dissatisfied people with huge egos who are only happy when they are considered the best," Tessa suggested. "Ignore them. You're surrounded by loving friends."

After another two hours of chat, Claire and the Corgis walked the guests to the door wishing everyone a goodnight.

Nicole hugged her friend tight. "You aren't allowed to solve a case without me ever again. I'm your back-up, remember? From now on, you are not authorized to make a move on a case without me."

Claire chuckled and promised she would follow Nicole's rules whenever working on a mystery.

"Don't ever go into a building alone again,

Blondie." Tony hugged her so tightly she lost her breath for a moment. "Got that? I don't want to lose you."

Ian was the last one in the line out the door. He paused. "Are you going to walk the dogs before you turn in?"

"I could. Would you like to go along?"

Ian smiled broadly. "You must be psychic. How else would you know I was angling for a walk?" he kidded.

Claire got the leashes while the Corgis danced around eager to go outside for the walk. Ian held Bear's lead and Claire took Lady's and the four strolled the neighborhood streets under the lamplights.

"We need to step up our training," Ian said. "We've been slacking lately."

"Ever the exercise tyrant." Claire laughed. "It's okay to take a break, you know."

"Well, if we take a break then I don't get to see you."

A rush of warmth bubbled through Claire's veins. She looked at Ian out of the corner of her eye. "Just so you know, I *am* willing to do other things with you besides run, bike, and swim."

A smile crept over Ian's lips. "That's good to know."

The Corgis yipped their approval when Ian reached down and took Claire's hand in his ... as those little zips of electricity flashed between them.

THANK YOU FOR READING!

Books by J.A. WHITING can be found here:
www.amazon.com/author/jawhiting

To hear about new books and book sales, please sign up for my mailing list at:
www.jawhitingbooks.com

Your email will never be sold, shared, or spammed.

If you enjoyed the book, please consider leaving a review. A few words are all that's needed. It would be very much appreciated.

BOOKS/SERIES BY J. A. WHITING

***CLAIRE ROLLINS COZY MYSTERY SERIES**

***PAXTON PARK COZY MYSTERIES**

***LIN COFFIN COZY MYSTERY SERIES**

***SWEET COVE COZY MYSTERY SERIES**

***OLIVIA MILLER MYSTERY-THRILLER SERIES**
(not cozy)

ABOUT THE AUTHOR

J.A. Whiting lives with her family in New England. Whiting loves reading and writing mystery stories.

Visit me at:

www.jawhitingbooks.com
www.facebook.com/jawhitingauthor
www.amazon.com/author/jawhiting